Dusk Till Dawn
in the
Wild World

Dusk Till Dawn
in the
Wild World

GRACE LARSON

Dusk Till Dawn in the Wild World

Copyright © 2022 by Grace Larson. All rights reserved.

No part of this publication may be reproduced, stored in a retrieval system or transmitted in any way by any means, electronic, mechanical, photocopy, recording or otherwise without the prior permission of the author except as provided by USA copyright law.

The opinions expressed by the author are not necessarily those of URLink Print and Media.

1603 Capitol Ave., Suite 310 Cheyenne, Wyoming USA 82001
1-888-980-6523 | admin@urlinkpublishing.com

URLink Print and Media is committed to excellence in the publishing industry.

Book design copyright © 2022 by URLink Print and Media. All rights reserved.

Published in the United States of America

Library of Congress Control Number: 2022902214
ISBN 978-1-68486-095-1 (Paperback)
ISBN 978-1-68486-096-8 (Digital)

28.01.22

Contents

Prologue...7
Death's Bitter Sting...9
The Legend Of The Big Draw.................................14
The All-American Family..17
Montana's Frontier..20
The Resurrected Cat..22
Our Dreams Cannot Be Our Children' Dreams.......24
Wild Horses..27
Orphan Foals..34
The Sheep Shed..39
Our Old House...43
Childhood Fears...47
Reflection...49
The Good Old Days...52
Change...56
Accident Prone...60
My Diverse Occupations..64
Spring On The Poloson Ranch...............................69
Impatience..74
The 8 Decades I Have Lived..................................77
Post Cards & Letters..99
The Poloson Place - 1929....................................117
Epilogue...119

Prologue

In Memory Of My Husband, Lyle "Bud" Larson
January 1, 1936 December 16, 2013

Loved One's Return

Death is like Yesterday
gone but not forgotten,
Memories come by day,
or with my dreams at night,
Prayer brings light,
knowledge, and insight,
Brilliant is our mind
blessings abound,
The Lord is kind
My dreams are so real
waking me as I feel
the closeness
we once had
of this I am so glad

The happiest years of my life were spent with
my Handsome Brown Eyed Man.

The title "Dusk To Dawn In The Wild World" is
compliments of my granddaughter, Virginia
Belle Oellrich.

Death's Bitter Sting

Photo from Cattle Today

WARMTH FROM THE SMALL WOOD stove filled the room but not quickly enough to suit Cal. He'd never been so cold. His slim body was defenseless against the harsh winter winds. Gnarled, aching hands tried to coax the fire but it stubbornly refused to burn with any intensity. With disgust, he gave up and accepted the warmth it gave.

Foggy glasses obscured his vision. In search of a handkerchief, he groped his way through the untidy room. The snow on his cap began to melt, dripping and running off his thin nose. Swiping at it, he swore,"God damn these Wyoming winters, looking after a bunch of starving cows in this God forsaken country is downright lunacy."

Again, he prodded the fire," wood must be wet,"he mumbled. A frown added more wrinkles to his weathered forehead. Cal was a small man, only five-eight with a body so thin that it appeared frail. His hollow blue eyes stared into the flames. For a while, he forgot the cold as his thoughts turned to the past.

This ranch was never his idea. Tired of his daughter's endless struggle to eek a living from truck stop restaurants, Shane Andrew had given them this small place. That was right after the war in '45. Ranching was new to Cal; he'd never really done much with his life. His only accomplishment was the army and all that had kept him in there was fear of a court martial.

Margaret's strong will and ambition made up for Cal's lack of purpose.So did her 20 years of ranch experience.Her mother had left her with Shane when she divorced him.Wyoming was too cold and isolated for Mrs. Andrew.

Margaret learned everything about ranching as she accompanied her father about the ranch, but her thoughts constantly turned to the fascination of Lander with its convenience; where electricity and a bathtub awaited her if she went to work at Ray's Truck Stop. Her father became very angry every time he thought of her desire to work away from home, but what could he do with a 25 year old daughter who was set in her ways? She'd gone to work at the truck stop waiting tables and that's where she met Cal Hamilton.

Shane Andrew never got over her marriage to Cal. He said of Cal," A City Dude who knows nothing about cattle, and doesn't even know how to work." Shane wanted his daughter to move home but she refused. Finally he persuaded her by giving her the small place that bordered his ranch. Cal hated Margaret's father.

Brooding had taken over Cal's life. He couldn't let go of the past; he sat sullen for a while, bitter thoughts churning through his head. The fire was dying down so he threw more wood on the coals then removed his mackinaw and chaps.He tugged at his boots, pulling them from his cold aching feet.

He thought about food but right now he needed some Jim Beam. Kicking an empty can out of the way, he headed for the whiskey cabinet. Cal counted the bottles; 13 left. That would last him until that snow plow came through. The whiskey festered his hostility. He hated the cattle and the letters he got from the bank. By spring, this place would be the bank's anyway. If any of the cattle survived, they would sell for enough to finance him for a little while.

The place was prospering when Margaret was alive. They had built dams, fences, and the new barn. In '45, a few scrawny Holstein-Hereford cross cows started their herd. By 1950, with the help of Sammy, Shane Andrew's purebred Hereford bull, their herd numbered 300 head.

"If only she were alive this house would be warm, supper ready, and my life one hell of a lot more tolerable," Cal muttered. He wanted to remember only the good times, but invariably no matter how hard he tried to fantasize, his thoughts seem to drift to their heated arguments; he couldn't drink enough to forget the last one. The trip to Lander for baler parts ended in a drunk.

When he hadn't returned home by supper time, Margaret drove into Lander. After searching all the bars, she found him in the Cody Inn.

"Damn you Cal Hamilton, you are an undependable, despicable rat! My father was right about you! This is it, I'm moving to Dad's, goodbye!" She had turned and stomped out, every bit of her 125 pounds filled with fury.

"Damn that woman doesn't she know I need some time away from that place, and besides that I have earned it," Cal had raged. He wasn't about to bow to her in front of the guys in the Cody Inn.

The next morning was filled with misery for Cal; he woke up smelling his own vomit. His pickup was disabled with a flat tire and every station in Lander was closed on Sunday; even the bars were closed. He dragged his aching body from the truck, staggering towards the spare tire and jack. With each step, his head threatened to split open. The ride home was a nightmare as the old pickup rattled and rocked over the rutted road. The baler parts were forgotten; all that mattered was his aching head and wretching stomach.

He noticed the vacant spot where the big truck was always parked. "God damned if she didn't mean it," remarked Cal. He'd think about her tomorrow. Right now his craving was aimed at the bottle of Jim Beam stashed beneath the front porch.

The next morning he drove to Shane Andrew's. He'd sooner take a beating but it didn't look like she was coming home of her own accord. Whiskey gave him courage. " She's my wife. Let her Old Man tried to keep her and I'll kill him."

Theirs was a marriage made of fire, flared by his whiskey, and so far the anger was always drowned in the passion of their lust. Somehow, he would cajole her with promises of total abstinence.

Sky, Margaret's dog, met him at the front gate. Cal hesitated, then reeled forward aiming his body in the direction of the big front door. Shane Andrew answered the door, "What the hell do you want! My daughter's had enough of your kind so get the hell off my place!"

Shane was over 6 feet tall and weighed at least 200 pounds. Putting his head foreword, Cal tried to knock him aside. Shane picked him up like a small dog, slapped him a few times, and set him in the pickup."You ever come near my daughter again and I'll break your rotten neck. Now get off my land and stay off," shouted Mr. Andrew.

The old Chevy started with a roar; shoving his foot down on the gas feed, Cal backed out of the yard, throwing gravel in all directions. That ornery old son of a bitch, I should have driven right through his house. If it hadn't been for him, Margaret and I would have made it fine," Cal said to himself.

Cal sat as close to the fire as he could; the whiskey was taking control. The fire was dying down and darkness was creeping in. The cattle wouldn't be fed tonight. Cal drifted into a fitful sleep; nightmares hounded him constantly. It was his fault that Margaret was dead. If only she was still here. He tossed about on the bed rumpling the dirty linens. Margaret was driving the big truck, careening down the mountain road. All at once it skidded on the ice, veered sideways, and rolled end over end down the side of the pass bursting into flames. Fitfully, he reached out,"I've got to get closer, get help," he said aloud.

The truth was tormenting him even within his sleep. He had been in Lander when she was killed. The day of the funeral, he was so drunk her father wouldn't allow him access to the funeral parlor or the cemetery.

Crawling out of bed, Cal stumbled towards the door and peered out. "I can reach her now. Wait a minute, Margaret, and I'll put out the fire." The cold cut deeper into his tormented soul as he lurched towards the burning truck.

Sam Norton found him when he plowed the road.

The Legend Of The Big Draw

My Grandparent's ranch was 8 miles from Niarada. We would frequently trade at the store.

This Legend is interesting to me because to travel to my Grandparent's ranch, one had to drive through the Big Draw.

The legend of the Big Draw always frightened me as a child growing up in the greater Flathead Lake area. If we went to Grandma and Grandpa's we had to go through The Big Draw, and frequently back through it to home at night. Below I share with you one version of the Legend of the Big Draw by Maggie Plummer from her blog Maggie's Musings. Think twice before trying to find this one at night.

The following story of the legend of the Big Draw was republished with permission from Maggie Plummer the author.

Things That Go "POOF!" in the Night...

Just a few miles west of Flathead Lake, the windblown sagebrush country around Niarada is like another world. In fact, some believe it is other-worldly.

The rolling land seems empty, and nightfall brings an inky blackness – the type that ghost stories are made of. Sure enough, the place is crawling with tales of a haunted tavern, a ghostly mother, a vanishing hitchhiker, and a headless horsewoman.

Niarada, pronounced to rhyme with "Nevada," is just a wide spot in the road these days. But it has a way of scaring the daylights out of folks, and many of them won't travel alone after dark on the remote stretches of road between here and Elmo.

Years ago there was a popular watering hole here called the Long Branch Bar. It was the kind of place known to host rattlesnake barbecues, Halloween bashes, impromptu rodeos, big dances, and – ghosts.

Most of the spooky stories center on Niarada's neighborhood ghost, "Hannah." One Long Branch bartender used to refuse to work at night because she was convinced that the building was haunted. One night as she was closing the bar, she kept trying to turn the lights off and they kept coming back on. Another night, she said, Hannah leaned on her car's horn, making it blast even though the vehicle's battery was supposed to be dead. Other stories had Hannah the ghost trying to suffocate someone with a pillow, or stomping around the kitchen.

Rancher Tom McDonald's Hannah story is the original, and most convincing, one. There was this old root cellar on his property, dug to store vegetables for a busy stagecoach stop, restaurant, and inn that used to be located there. Even though many, many years have passed since weary travelers stopped there, and the two-story inn has long since surrendered to the elements, the cellar remains.

And so does its ghost, according to McDonald and many others.

About 50 years ago now, one of McDonald's ranch hands spent a night in the root cellar, then said the next day that he'd spoken with a strange woman and her two little girls, and that all of them had worn old-fashioned long skirts and aprons. The woman's name was Hannah, he claimed. Again and again he saw the woman and her girls come up out of that root cellar. One time he tried to shake Hannah's hand, and she and the girls abruptly turned and went down the cellar stairs, quickly disappearing.

Folks were pretty skeptical until one day when McDonald was getting a haircut in Polson and happened to visit with an old-timer there. When the elderly man realized McDonald was from Niarada, he began talking about other old-timers from that area. McDonald asked him about the old stage stop on his place and the man said it had been run by some people named Flagg. When McDonald asked him what Mrs. Flagg's first name was, the man answered, "Hannah." How many children did the Flaggs have, the rancher asked. "Two daughters," the old-timer replied.

McDonald began giving his ranch hand's stories more credence. But then he had to cover up the cellar so his cows wouldn't fall in. He wondered if the ghosts were trapped in there. He didn't mind having a ghost on his place, he said, as long as it left him alone. McDonald was used to ghost stories, he would say, having grown up hearing them from the Indians.

He believed that the Flathead Reservation is full of haunted places like his cellar.

But a lot of folks think the Niarada neighborhood is particularly spooky.

They've heard stories about a vanishing hitchhiker, or headless horsewoman, along Montana Highway 28 between Niarada and Elmo. That's an area called "The Big Draw," a tunnel-like valley that still doesn't have electrical lines. The handful of people who live there use generators.

Not everyone is scared. Some intrepid types go out to the Big Draw at night looking for the headless horsewoman. Or the hitchhiking woman who disappears without a trace.

Who are these apparitions? Could they be Hannah Flagg, tired of her lonely root cellar and looking for some company?

No one seems to know.

The All-American Family

MR, AND MRS WILLIS DECIDED that their sons needed to live in a very nice house in the most influential part of Spokane. The boys could concentrate on their schoolwork if they didn't have too many chores, and Fred Willis certainly wanted his sons to make their living with brains and not brawn. Mrs. Willis had never worked away from home because that wasn't her idea of a good mother. Unfortunately, the Willis household didn't run any better than the Jones' house down the street. Both parents worked and their boys had free run of the town.

It is Tuesday morning at the Willis home; Fred and Mary are trying to sleep in because this happens to be the only day Fred has off this week. "The boys are at it again, Mary! Can't they ever quit fighting for just one morning?"

"I know how you feel, Fred, but I gave up long ago. I just close my ears and my mind to it. If I didn't, I'd go insane in a week if not a day."

Fred said, "They are sure thankless for all the sacrifices we have made to bring them up in this neighborhood. When I was a boy, we carried wood and water, slopped hogs, and milked cows. We had to be at the school bus stop by 7 AM or get left. Maybe we made a mistake by moving into this neighborhood and letting the boys off easy. At our old place they had quite a bit more to do."

"Maybe you are right, Fred. Let's think about selling this place and buying that run down farm out by my folks' place. The boys would have so much work to do that they wouldn't have time to fight all the time."

"Hey, that's an excellent idea, Mary! Why didn't we think of that sooner. Just think, ten more years of rest and relaxation, but I guess it's not too late to start now. We will tell the boys tonight and I'm calling your Mom and telling her we will soon be her new neighbors."

Craig and John had no idea what their parents had cooked up while they were in school. Both boys sauntered into the house with their usual greetings for one another.

"Well boys, Fred said, we have a big surprise for you. Your mother and I bought the old Keller place and we're moving next month."

"You are kidding", Dad, said Craig.

"No, I am not kidding. Your mother and I have gotten fed up with you boys having so much idle time to play and fight, and we are just sick and tired of trying to keep up with the Jones."

Craig said," Just wait until I get my hands on John!"

John said, "Just a minute, Craig, I don't start all the fights around here!

Craig said,"No, but you start enough of them and I'm going to lay you lower than a snake for this. The next thing you know we will be cleaning barns, milking cows, and that place doesn't even have running water in the house."

John said," Yes Craig, you're going to stink when you pick Becky up. Your jock image will be shot down the tube. The more I think about Dad's idea, the better I like it. When are we moving, Dad?"

Montana's Frontier

I HAVE ALWAYS BEEN FASCINATED BY Montana's early days. The Missouri Badlands constituted one of the loneliest of all lands. No homesteaders ventured into this rugged domain. Thousands of acres uninhabited by farmers or domestic animals.

Roads and trails were almost impassable. Scrub pine and cedar grew in shadowed coulees, below the hills which started up from the canyon floors.

Here, in the 1880's, an organization of renegades, ex buffalo hunters, fur traders, southern bushwhackers, and murderers established their headquarters. So complete, did they rule the breaks, that law abiding men didn't dare venture forth on the dim trails, nor did any detachment of U.S. Troops ever invade this Robbers' Roost of Montana.

Half breed trappers of bobcats, wolves, lions, and coyotes inhabited the ranges. This was the best region in the state because fur bearing animals were plentiful, although Montana wasn't as famous as some of the more watered states that were in the fur industry.

The first steamboat reached Ft. Benton on July 2, 1860. The American Fur Trade Company steamboats, Chippewa and Keywest, arrived at the trading post of Ft. Benton. With the boats came wood choppers, as the steamboats needed fuel to navigate the Missouri.

Many of the wood cutters were killed by marauding Indians. As the woodsmen moved on to seek other work, the wolfers moved in. These men were tougher than the buffalo hunter. They could make several thousand dollars from a season's hunt. in 1884, the first statewide bounty law was passed in Montana. That first year, 5,450 wolf hides were presented for payment. All but three Montana counties reported a bounty payment for wolves from 1900–1931 (Riley 1998).

1884-1923, 39 years until the famous white wolf, Lady Snowdrift, was finally shot on Dexter Creek in 1923. According to the Helena-Lewis and Clark National Forest's website. Soon after that, Old Snowdrift was caught in a trap baited with her scent. "He had been living right in town to begin with," said Dennis Driscoll, a retired teacher involved with the Kane history group. "That pack could be the last of the pure wolves left in America."

The excerpts for this story are from notes I found in my mother's treasures. She passed away in 2008, and was born into an Immigrant and Homesteader family in 1923.

The Resurrected Cat

WE WENT TO THE BARN to feed on a snowy winter morning. We had a big stack of bales that we fed the horses from. We were shocked to see a half eaten rabbit stuck in the haystack. My husband said, " that is it, that gray cat has to go." Lyle and I finished the chores, went in and had breakfast, then Lyle took the 22 and went after the gray cat. Lyle shot the gray female and returned to the house.

We were eating lunch when a gray cat jumped up on the window sill. My husband's expression was absolutely the funniest thing I have ever seen; he almost tipped his chair over. Lyle said, I am sure that I killed that cat so how could she be looking in the window at me? I was still laughing because of the way Lyle reacted to the resurrected cat.

Image by Renate Gellings-Reese from Pixabay

Our Resurrected Cat

After some searching we figured out there were two cats and both were gray. This gray cat was given a reprieve. He was a beat up old male full of battle scars, and he had been a house cat at one time. We were careful not to let him in the house in fear that he would spray his scent, and he also beat on our spade female. We named him Bob because his tail was only about an inch long. The one time he did get into the house, Lyle was opening a can with the electric can opener, and Bob came asking for food. He was in the house; what a surprise.

Bob would disappear for weeks at a time. He came home with a snare tightly wrapped around his belly. Lyle remove the snare and doctored his wound. Bob became very dear to us as he would ride in the wheelbarrow, and he loved to be carried all over on our shoulders, and he kept our female cat in the house. Millie was a bird killer; she was scared of Bob so didn't even try to go outside.

The next time Bob came home he was in pretty good shape and resumed riding in the wheelbarrow and following us everywhere we went, and asking to be carried. The next time Bob disappeared he came home badly wounded. His wounds were such that we had to take him to the vet; he had a big gash on his throat and he was pretty sick. Bob healed up from that and took off again. Each time Bob disappeared we thought we'd never see him again, but for at least five years Bob came and went until, finally, he used up all of his nine lives. We were sad when Bob didn't come back again.

This led to freedom for Milly and she would get out every chance she got. Once I rescued a baby rabbit and another time, a Meadowlark. We really missed Bob because he was our cat guard, and Millie didn't dare go outside while Bob was around.

Our Dreams Cannot Be Our Children' Dreams

I HAD KAHILL GIBRAN'S LITTLE BOOK years ago, and what I recall is his writings on our children's futures.

On Children
Kahlil Gibran–1883-1931

And a woman who held a babe against her bosom said, Speak to us of Children.

And he said:

Your children are not your children.

They are the sons and daughters of Life's longing for itself.

They come through you but not from you,

And though they are with you yet they belong not to you.

You may give them your love but not your thoughts,

For they have their own thoughts.

You may house their bodies but not their souls,

For their souls dwell in the house of tomorrow, which you cannot visit, not even in your dreams.

You may strive to be like them, but seek not to make them like you.

For life goes not backward nor tarries with yesterday.

You are the bows from which your children as living arrows are sent forth.

The archer sees the mark upon the path of the infinite, and He bends you with His might that His arrows may go swift and far.

Let your bending in the archer's hand be for gladness;

For even as He loves the arrow that flies, so He loves also the bow that is stable.

From The Prophet (Knopf, 1923). This poem is in the public domain.

I had been to Spokane to visit my son, Dan's, adult children. On the way home I thought of Kahill Gibran's writings on children, and how his words apply to my relationship with my children and grandchildren today.

We want our children to be more successful in life than we were. And even with my grandchildren, I want that same success in their lives. My children and grandchildren have far
surpassed what I have achieved in my lifetime of 80 years.

Dan's son and his wife are exploring Western Washington just as Lyle and I did almost 40 years ago. Kettle Falls, Spokane's Parks, and its famous Merry Go Round. The beautiful Spokane River that runs on to the Columbia, and Hawk Falls where Dan scared us when he took the canoe so far out into the river. The streets Lyle and I drove, and Dan drove as he delivered flowers for Jean.

As I watched the joy my Grandson and his wife share, it made my heart sing a happy song.

I pray that they are just as happy, and pleased with the happiness they have found. Sadly, Lyle and Dan are no longer with us.

Dan's widow and daughter, Dan's youngest, have moved to Spokane where they will also share some of the very things Lyle and I did.

Each generation has accomplished more than the previous generation, as it should be. As I watched my Grandchildren, I was amazed at how responsible they are, and how involved they are in helping others.

My definition of success is: being fulfilled, happy, safe, healthy, and loved. It is the ability to strive for your goals whatever those goals may be. My Grandchildren are living successful lives.

Let your bending in the archer's hand be for gladness;

For even as He loves the arrow that flies, so He loves also the bow that is stable.

Life for my children was anything but stable. The next generation created the stability I was unable to have for my children. But my bending in the archer's hand is for Gladness for my children and grandchildren and their journey through life here on our beautiful earth.

Their hopes and dreams are their own, and I am glad for them. " For their souls dwell in the house of tomorrow, which you cannot visit, not even in your dreams. "

Wild Horses

Przewalski's Horse

It is said that the only true wild horse is the Przewalski's horse. It has long been considered the only remaining non-domesticated wild horse. A 2018 DNA study suggested that modern Przewalski's horses may descend from allegedly domesticated horses of the Botai culture. However, a 2021 study came to the conclusion that the Botai horses were wild Przewalski's horses and not domesticated. wikipedia.org The Botai culture is an archaeological culture (c. 3700–3100 Bc) of prehistoric north-western Asia. It was named after the settlement of Botai in today's northern Kazakhstan.

The Przewalski's horse of Central Asia became extinct in the wild in 1969. However, over the past few centuries feral horses have been introduced to all continents except Antarctica, and Przewalski's horses have been reintroduced to their former habitats in Mongolia.

Montana Feral Horses

My mother, Marie Poloson, told me about the wild horses that were back of the Poloson Ranch when she was a girl. That would have been the early 1930's. She would take oats and spread the grain on a flat rock; the horses would come as soon as they saw Mom knowing they had a treat.

John Rhone had a write up on the Feral Horses that roamed the Flathead Reservation. This was in the Hot Springs Citizen dated

May 30, 1968. He said the actual wild horses had been rounded up right after the Reservation opened to Homesteading in 1910. His thoughts were that the horses that were grazing in the hills were those let loose by their owners, and stray mares the Feral Stallions would steal from a ranchers herd. He did not believe there were any truly wild horses left, only Feral Horses. My mother would not agree.

The dictionary description of Feral : "an animal in a wild state, especially after escape from captivity or domestication."

The Pryor Mountain Mustangs

The Pryor Mountain wild horses have been traced back to the Colonial Spanish Horse using DNA testing. The Colonial Spanish Horse is now a Heritage Breed. The Pryor Mustangs originated from the Colonial Spanish horse, but not all feral horses of the Americas today are of Colonial Spanish descent. There has been considerable crossbreeding in some areas. The Colonial Spanish breed comes from the feral populations that were raised in the Iberian Peninsula; this peninsula separates Spain from Portugal.

Pryor Mountain Mustangs are relatively small horses, usually 14 hands although some are taller or shorter. A hand is 4 inches so a 14 hand horse stands 56 inches. Pryor Mountain Mustangs exhibit a natural ambling gait, and domesticated Pryor Mountain Mustangs are known for their strength, sure-footedness and stamina. Some of the Mustangs have a Dorsal Stripe that runs down their back, and zebra stripes on their legs. These markings aren't always present on each Pryor Mountain Mustang, though all of them have a dorsal stripe and and nearly all have distinct leg stripes. The colors vary; duns of various shades, grullo, buckskin, bay, black, sorrel, chestnut, and red and blue roan. Palominos are rare. Medicine Bow was the last Pryor horse to show the sabino color pattern.

Photo Courtesy Of Joseph C. Filer

This is one of many wonderful photos Joseph Filer has taken of the Pryor Mountain Mustangs.

My late husband & I made many trips to the Pryor Mountains to see the wild horses. They came right up to our camp once. They are curious and as long as all is still they have a need to check it out.

It is believed that the wild horses have been in the Pryors since the late 17th century. The Native Tribes owned hundreds of these wild horses. When the pioneers arrived there were thousands of wild horses in Montana and Wyoming. Ranch raised stallions were turned loose to breed with the wild mares; this cross resulted in tough horses for the Cavalry.

War Horses

My book, Fay, tells the stories of her husband, Bill Haynes, as he trained these horses for the Military. This was in Northern Montana near Babb in the late 1930's and early 1940's.

And in 1941, Life magazine reported that the U.S. Army was supplying itself with 20,000 horses. In fact, according to the magazine, it was the biggest order for horses the army had placed since the Civil War. On the battlefield, cavalry made a number of contributions during World War II. Horses were still used in the war in Afghanistan.

Protecting The Wild Horses & Burros

The wild horses were not protected by law until the Wild Horse Annie Act prohibited the use of automobiles and motor vehicles to chase and capture wild horses. In 1964, the BLM declared that it would remove all the Pryor Mountain wild horses and disperse them through auctions, an initiative that spurred widespread public opposition. This temporarily delayed the movement against these horses. By 1968, these animals were mostly limited to the BLM lands due to the construction of fences and earlier roundups. In the same year, the BLM again concentrated on removing the herd, but with a possibility of returning 15-35 horses to the range. Concerned with the fate of these animals, the PMWHA (Pryor Mountain Wild Horse Association) was established. It worked with other organizations including the ISPA to prevent the roundup.

The tussle around the Pryor Mountain horses continued until the enactment of the The Wild Free-Roaming Horses and Burros Act in 1971. This Act prevented killing or harassing of wild burros and horses on federal land, habits and habitats, as well as authorized public land for their use. The Act was jointly administered by the US Forest Service and the BLM.

The Bureau of Land Management (BLM), has set the optimum Pryor Mustang Herd number at 120 animals. Genetic studies have revealed that the herd exhibits a high degree of genetic diversity and a low degree of inbreeding, and BLM has acknowledged the genetic uniqueness of the herd.

The Plight Of The Wild Horses & Burros

Today, there are over 95,000 wild horses and burros. National appropriate level is said to be 27,000 horses & burros. Total on range excess are 61,400 horses & burros.

Today, some 36,000 wild horses are awaiting their fate in holding facilities such as the Palomino Valley in Nevada, and Susanville in northern California. Four-year contracts have been awarded to private ranchers in Oklahoma and Kansas to manage long-term holding facilities.

Rock Springs Wild Horse Holding Facility is the only federal off-range corral and preparation facility in Wyoming. The facility houses approximately 800 wild horses, primarily gathered from Wyoming herd management areas. The facility also serves as a rest stop location for wild horses being transported eastbound from western states.

Currently there are 35 pasture facilities in 9 states with a combined acreage of approximately 330,000, and a combined horse & burro capacity of about 38,000. Current pasture population about 36,500 horses & burros. The program is currently preparing another pasture solicitation targeting the states of OK/KS/NE seeking ranches with capacity to hold 1,000-10,000 head. Planned posting date was November 2019.

Public Off-Range Pastures (PORPs):

Wind River Ranch, Lander, WY – 940 acres – 225 head capacity

Deerwood Ranch, Laramie, WY – 4,700 acres – 350 head capacity

Mowdy Ranch, Coalgate, OK – 3,500 acres – 350 head capacity

Montana's Wild Horse Sanctuary is 500 acres. They are funded by grants and donations. They offer professionally trained Mustangs for adoption.

Madeleine Pickens giant ranch, in northeastern Nevada, is spread across three valleys and two mountain ranges, and Pickens intends to turn it all into a wild-horse sanctuary, or as she calls it, Mustang Monument. The first arrivals are 500 horses she bought from a Paiute Indian reservation. The horses, she says, would otherwise have been slaughtered across the border in Mexico.

RANGE Magazine had a letter from Veterinarian John E. Radosevich of Rock Springs, WY. He said he is predicting a death loss of 10 to 20 percent of feral horses through this Summer and Fall. They are hauling water by helicopter to the wildlife. 50,000 horses, or however many there are, will need 500,000 gallons of water every day. How is this even possible ? Congress makes a rule that the feral horse shall not be slaughtered for anything, including feed for big cats, predator birds and sporting dogs, let alone human consumption. The Malthusian Theory is about to be proven. Malthusian theory– Malthus' theory that population increase would outpace increases in the means of subsistence. In other words grass and water in the horse and burro world. Areas that have been overgrazed now have Cheatgrass which is a weed. Cheatgrass is one of the most highly invasive weeds found in the colder parts of the country. Once the seeds germinate, the roots develop very quickly and are fully developed as early as spring. It has often been reported to infest newly seeded areas.

Feral wild horses also cost the U.S. a lot of money. To manage wild horses, the Forest Service and the Bureau of Land Management have to cover both on-range populations and off-range holding costs. The estimated "lifetime" cost of keeping a wild horse in off-range pastures or holding facilities is $50,000 per animal. In 2019 alone, the bureau spent nearly $50 million caring for wild horses. How long do horses live in captivity? Depending on its breed, management and environment, the modern domestic horse has a life expectancy of 25 to 30+ years, regardless of breed.

What are the answers for these beautiful horses and cute burros? I was born on a horse, sheep, and cattle ranch. I cried when a horse died or had to be put down. One still holds a very sad memory because that stallion was the best horse I ever rode, whether bareback or with a saddle, we covered hundreds of miles during his lifetime.

But, if I were a horse and had to be locked up in a holding pen with several hundred other horses, each searching for dominance. Horses accept dominance when we or another animal cause them to move when they prefer not to. Or another animal inhibits movement when they want to flee. There is little room to flee the dominant horses in these pens ! Stallions in a herd usually cause continued chaos as they fight each other for dominance. This is no way to live whether it is a wild burro or a wild horse. If I, as a horse, could not find a home, I would choose to be put to death other than to be imprisoned in the holding pen forever!

That brings about another problem. Because Congress ruled that these horses and burros could not be slaughtered, all the HUMANE slaughtering plants were closed. Now, horses are transported to Mexico or Canada, and their methods, are they HUMANE? And is it humane to let these beautiful animals die because they haven't any water or grass? When the pools of water become low they become infested with the Algae growth which causes the horses to drink less and it can be toxic. Add the manure mixed with the mud in these very low sources of water is so harmful to the wild horses. Parasites such as Tape Worms and other worms thrive in these conditions.

Do we want these beautiful wild horses and burros dying of thirst and starvation? Maybe those who truly love these animals need to contact Congress and see if Humane Slaughter Plants can be opened again in the United States.

My heart hurts when I think of slaughtering a horse but it hurts worse when I see them dying from thirst and starvation.

Orphan Foals

UTERINE HEMORRHAGE, ONE OF THE most critical emergencies for a mare after foaling is hemorrhage of the uterine blood vessels. It is most common in older mares, and can result in death if not given immediate veterinarian care; and sometimes the very best care cannot save the mare. Joe's dam was 20 years old, and she had foaled many times over the years.

A phone call from Earl Jones changed our lives; very little sleep, goat's milk in the refrigerator, bottle washing, and no trips without a foal sitter.

Silvertip Joe was 16 days old when we met a friend who had brought him as far as Billings. He was withdrawn and didn't seem to care for humans. Earl had told us he had worked, very carefully, with Joe because he didn't want to spoil him.

Joe was foaled May 27, 1997. His Tennessee Walking Horse Breeders & Exhibitors registration number was 972394. Joe's sire: Shaker's Satan TWHBEA# 805965. His dam, Shadow Of Tegun TWHBEA# 773262. We already owned a half sister to Joe, Tegun's Mt Fawn. Fawn was not Imprinted but she spent her foal time with her dam. She wasn't pushed away by a human or even handled by one until she was weaned. Fawn had a gentle disposition and responded well to humans.

The 2 hour feedings gave us time to work with Joe, but he would not warm up to either one of us. We had started reading veterinarian, Robert Miller's book on "Imprinting The Newborn Foal." Joe didn't have any imprinting; he'd been repeatedly pushed away except for his bottle. Imprinting, to be successful, takes place as soon as the foal is born.

My Mother and Joe

We brushed Joe, lifted his feet, and trained him to lead. Interaction with the other horses was a daily part of his training. Joe was healthy and was eating hay and a grain ration when he became very sick. We took him to the vet for a diagnosis and treatment; stomach ulcers or injury from something he had eaten was the vet's best guess. Our driveway was being black topped and we were pretty sure he had eaten black top. We made the horse trailer into a hospital room for Joe, and he did recover. Lyle said he had expected to find a dead Joe every time he arrived home from work.

Teaching Joe to lead

Even with all the doctoring Joe did not warm up to humans. Nurturing must be as critical for an orphan foal as it is for an infant.

Joe was sold to a man in Wyoming and the last we heard he was in Texas. How he was responding was never known to us. Hopefully, he was enjoying good care and a useful life.

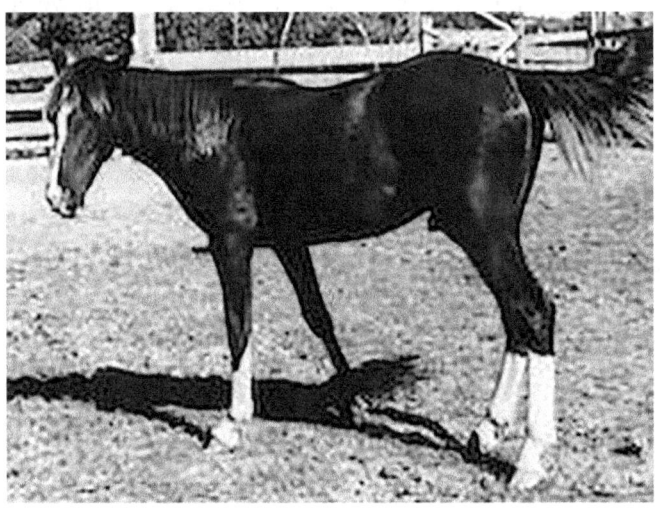

Weanling Joe

On 9-9-99, at 2 AM, a call came asking if we would take an orphan filly. Roy's mare had died and he had no way of caring for the foal we named "Boo." I told him we would take her if he would give her to us. Feedings every 2 hours again!

Boo didn't get any colostrum from her Dam so we went to the feed store. They had an artificial colostrum powder that would get Boo protected with the antibodies needed for her to survive.

She was the most lovable filly, and we became so attached to her.

After the much needed powdered colostrum, Boo was given goat's milk. Our neighbors raised goats; we would buy it from them by the gallon. It was kept in the refrigerator; more than once, Lyle would grab a gallon, take a swig, and head for the sink to spit out the goat's milk ! And to think babies used to drink goat's milk. It is one of the healthiest sources of milk for humans and baby animals. Cow's milk tends to cause diarrhea in foals.

We were invited to Yellowstone Park by friends; a stay in the beautiful Lodge too. Boo would have to go to the Veterinarian's for care while we were gone. I turned my back and Boo was gone ! We looked everywhere for her. When we finally found her she was badly injured. The neighbor's dog, a Rottweiler, had chased her, biting her all over. Thankfully, Boo never fell or was tackled to the ground.

Our trip was off, and Boo was on her way to the Vet. We made a hospital room out of the horse trailer again. 24 hour care brought Boo through this and she trusted us; a bond developed between her and Lyle. When he'd start the Ford Tractor, Boo would be ready to race. We had Boo until she was 2 years then sold her to a family in ND. She would race their tractor too.

Boo never developed any pushy behaviors. She was always lovable and willing to do what was asked of her. There was a world of difference between Boo, the nurtured orphan, and Joe, the orphan kept at a distance.

Boo turned out to be a beautiful trail mare. Her owner took her on trail rides in North Dakota and Montana, and would stop for a visit on her way by our place.

Boo meets the big horses

Boo and Lyle

The Sheep Shed

The Old Sheep Shed

THE LAST TIME THE SHEEP were in this shed was during lambing in 1962. That was the last year my Grandfather, Dan Poloson, raised sheep.

His and Grandma's dream started near Helena when he worked for the Herron sheep ranch. They saved for 11 years so they could buy the ranch in Rattlesnake Gulch. The ranch was made up of homesteads, the Vander Ende, the Carlin, the Howser, the Loder, and several others. The ranch was over 2000 acres with a Sagebrush Flat that was about 640 acres.

The sheep shed was 75 feet wide and 400 feet long. It was used during lambing and shearing.

A row of very small pens lined part of the south wall. These were used when the ewe would not let her lamb suck. Grandpa would get in the small pen with the ewe, hold her steady, and help the lamb find the teat. With 2000 ewes lambing, this was a 24 hour job. Grandpa would take short breaks, sleep for an hour or so, and go right back to work. He had several men working with him, and his herders when he took the sheep to the mountains.

A sheep eats 4 pounds of hay a day so 2000 head would eat almost 4 ton of hay. The ranch had 2 International trucks that hauled the hay; loose hay before baled hay was invented. The stacks in the hay yard were huge, and I often wondered how the men ever put the huge loads on the trucks.

The hay was alfalfa, and we chopped it for the ewes. There was very little waste with chopped hay. Feeding the sheep and cattle was done with a team of horses. The day was started with harnessing the team, giving them a treat of oats, then taking them out to where they were hooked up to the wagon. The chopped hay went directly onto the wagon. The team pulled the wagon along side feed troughs; we shoveled the hay into troughs. We would then load the loose hay onto the wagon for the cattle. As the team pulled the wagon along, Grandpa would pitch the hay to the cows.

A truck loaded with hay from the Lonepine valley farms, my uncle Bert and Leo Mountjoy standing proudly by their huge load of hay.

The ranch was busy during lambing, docking, dipping for ticks, castrating, and shearing. The Cookhouse always had big meals made for hard working appetites. The groceries were purchased at the Lonepine Store. 50 pound sacks of flour, 25 pound sacks of sugar, eggs, bacon, canned goods, etc.

The Shearers were a family that came every year. The shearing was always done in the sheep shed. The fleeces were packed in large burlap bags with a man using his weight to tamp the wool, then the bag was sewn shut. These held approximately 300 pounds of wool. These sacks were loaded onto our old International Truck, and off to the railroad for shipping. At that time Plains, Montana was the closest place to ship the wool.

Once the shearing was finished next was the dipping, docking the tails, and castrating. The sheep shed was not used until the next lambing, and shearing season. It was cleaned of the manure, and ready for the next year's activity. Once all the care was finished the ewes and lambs were herded to summer pasture in Idaho's St. Joe Forest.

The sheep shed came to a sad end with the Rattlesnake Gulch fire, September of 2018. Sheep hadn't used it since 1962; it had been vacant for 54 years. Someone said they wanted it named a Historical Building.

Some of my happy days were spent in that sheep shed. As the fire burned, I kept praying that the Old Sheep Shed would survive, and I was very sad when it burned.

Photo by By MTPR News

The sheep shed stands as the fire creeps closer and eventually takes its life.

Our Old House

My sister, Alice, and my Step Father, Debs, moving our old house.

MOM MARRIED WARREN DEBS MCBROOM in 1942. My sister, Alice, was born a year later. Debs was always "Daddy" to me. I did not even know my own father. I was four months short of three years when Alice was born.

World War II was in full force. Debs had three brothers in that war. My earliest memory was Debs setting by the table listening to the war news on the old radio. Ration stamps were needed for gas and groceries. We had one pair of shoes and they's better last. Mom and Debs raised chickens for eggs, and fryers, and they traded eggs for groceries. Our two cows named Jersey and Guernsey, provided milk and cream. The cream was separated into cream cans and sold to the Creamery in Polson.

Our old house was about 100 yards south of the barn, but that meant hauling water from the spring, a half mile below the house, up to the house for cooking, cleaning, laundry, and bathing. Our parents made the decision to move the house, so the spring water could gravity feed, instead of being hauled almost daily. A pipeline was buried deep enough so it wouldn't freeze, and now we were able to turn on the outside faucet, and fill a bucket with water. We had to carry the water about 30 feet to the house.

The old house was never painted; it had no insulation or indoor plumbing. The upstairs was divided into two rooms; both with wooden floors; slivers were common if we were barefoot. Alice and I had one room for our bedroom and the other was a store room.

Our window held a wonderful view of the valley, and Chief Cliff many miles in the distance. The Northern Lights were a beautiful sight during the winter. Thunder storms with flashes of lightening lit up the valley. That window, and its views, are a fond memory from well over 70 years ago.

The downstairs was also 2 big rooms. Mom and Debs took the south end for their bedroom, and the rest of the house held the kitchen and living room. Their bedroom had a wide shelf above the clothes closet. Mom would put me up there for my afternoon nap. I didn't like to take naps, and worst of all was listening to Mom's radio program, Helen Trent!

The wood cookstove's stovepipe went through a hole in the wall; chimney fires were frequent, either from a hot fire in the cookstove, or the wood heater that was connected to the same stove pipe. The old house never caught fire which was a miracle. The dry boards would have burned like kindling.

The stairway to our bedroom didn't have a railing. My earliest memory of that was walking off of our bedroom floor and landing at the bottom of the stairs. My arm dislocated so Debs carried me to the sofa, and proceeded to put my arm back into place. Very painful for a child of four.

When we started school at Big Arm, 7 miles from our old house, the road would be impassable due to mud in the spring or snow drifts in the winter. Many times during the long winters, Mom or Debs would have to come after us with the team and sled. When spring arrived the team would pull the old pickup through the muddy ruts in the road, and to better road conditions.

Not only was the old house uninsulated, but the windows weren't caulked. Snow would blow in around our bedroom window. Alice and I would crawl into bed with our clothes on; it just seemed too cold to change into night clothes. If we did take our clothes off the wasps always found a way to crawl into a pant leg, or a shirt sleeve. We were stung so many times. The bees liked to crawl inside our shoes too.

Mom and Debs raised a huge garden, raspberries, strawberries, and even gooseberries. One year, Debs decided to raise peanuts. He had the peanuts, he was using for seed in a box, in the spare bedroom. Alice and I discovered the peanuts and thought they were good to eat. By the time Debs discovered the loss of his peanuts, we had eaten almost all of them. I don't remember being punished.

The old house had a tin roof; rain falling on the roof made the most wonderful sound. It was easy to fall asleep while listening to it. That tin roof may have saved the old house during the frequent chimney fires.

The upstairs had a cubby hole area. jAn old crank phonograph was stored there. I liked to wind it up and play old records. I found "Old Shep" by Red Foley; I played it over and over. Each time I would cry. Maybe I thought Old Shep wouldn't die if I played it often enough. I was only 5 or 6 years old. Our pup, Wolf, had been ran over on Christmas morning, so that made the song about Shep even more poignant.

When Debs and Mom divorced the Old House became a very sad place for me and Alice. Our bedroom was cold before, but after he left it was freezing! Two sad girls went to bed every night, and went off to school every day.

The day came when Mom sold the place. Alice was staying with a family assisting with their children. I was staying at our

Grandparent's ranch. The Old House, and the ranch, we knew as children, left me with a forlorn feeling. The ranch, the horses, and the hills were so much a part of me.

When I was 16 I had my own car and made one last trip to the old house and ranch. The old house was bare except for an old bed that was upstairs in our bedroom, and the ranch no longer had cattle and horses. It was getting late when I drove up to the old house, so I decided to stay over night. I slept in my clothes on the bed that was left upstairs. It was one of the saddest times of my youth. The next morning I looked over the valley, for the last time, from my upstairs window.

Years later, I drove up the gravel road, far enough, so I could look up the valley of my childhood. The old house was gone. It was as if no one had ever lived there.

Childhood Fears

I WAS BORN IN 1940 WHEN WW II was in full swing. I recall the ration stamps, one pair of shoes, and limited gasoline and oil. My parents owned a ranch so oil and gas were vital. Parts for machinery were limited because all metals went towards the war machines. That's where the old saying, "held together with baling wire" comes from. For those who put up loose hay other methods had to be used.

My Step Father's brothers Dick, Jim, and Wes joined the military. My Step Father had Scarlet Fever so he wasn't eligible. His brother, Cliff, had lost a hand playing with dynamite. My parents went to every war movie that was ever made, I think. The Propaganda pieces made the Japanese and Germans incredibly scary. For a very young child, frightening. I wonder how many of my friends were afraid during that time?

My parents liked Westerns too. I must have been quite timid because I was so afraid. Everything seemed very real to me. Like the time Rita Hayworth was tied to a stake, and the Indians had set a fire beneath her. I started crying so Mom took me out of the theatre, sat me in the old pickup, and returned to watch the movie. All kinds of scary scenes were running through my mind.

Even, as a young adult, I would have dreams where the Japanese were after me. Propaganda sure worked on me!

I'm sure many of my friends have stories to tell about this time in their life. Maybe once this virus is behind us we can get together and share some of our childhood memories. I'm young in comparison to some of you. The Depression Years must have memories. Those of you who weathered those years and WW II, The Korean War, and Viet Nam may have lost loved ones. I heard today that 645,000 men and women died in the wars to date.

Reflection

ANN LAY ON HER BED with her mind in turmoil. Could she testify against her own Mother? Their ranch was going to be lost for sure. Her Mother's attorney would cost at least $5000. Ann loved the ranch with all of her heart and soul.

She mulled all the losses that would come into her life if the ranch was taken by the bank. She would not be able to race over the land bareback on her horse, Flame. And she would never again have the beautiful view of the valley that was especially splendid during thunder storms. The lightening flashes would light up the valley, the horses, and the cattle that grazed in the meadow. Even the smell of the alfalfa hay would be gone.

Ann's Mom had stolen a horse and altered the brand. Ann asked her not to do this, but her pleas fell on deaf ears. Ann's stepfather even asked her Mom to think of the consequences. It was like her mother was in a different world.

How did the Brand Inspector find out? Ann was told that the horse's owner had reported him missing. But, how did the search lead to Ann's Mom? The horse had been pastured at least 3 miles from Ann's Mother's ranch. Maybe someone watched as he was lead from his pasture.

A warrant was issued for her Mother's arrest. Bail was posted, and $5000 was borrowed from Ann's grandfather for the attorney. Ann had told her grandparents the truth about the brand being altered by her mother, their oldest daughter. Ann's grandmother would not believe that her own daughter could do such a thing.

Ann found out that her mother had told her Grandmother that the hired hand had altered the brand. Ann was shocked! Jason was only 15 years old. He had asked if he could stay at the ranch if he earned his keep. This was agreed upon and Jason had been helping on the ranch for over a year.

How could her Mother do such a thing? Jason had nothing to do with altering the brand. He hadn't even been present when it happened. Again, Ann tried to convince her Grandmother, but she could not accept that an unlawful deed had occurred at the hands of her daughter.

The court hearing was only a few days away. Ann knew she had to tell the truth if her Mother would not. There wasn't any way Jason would be blamed. Ann would see to that and she told her mother, "if you try to blame Jason, at the hearing, I will speak up loud and clear."

Ann moved to her Grandparent's ranch because she was afraid of her Mother's anger. Hair pulling or a switch would be her punishment if she stayed near her mother. To make matters even more painful, Ann had watched her Grandfather bow his head and cry. He was her Rock, and had always been there for her. It hurt so much to see his pain. It was especially bad because her Grandparents were so divided over her Mother's conduct.

Ann and her Grandfather went to the hearing. When Ann's Mother saw them she must have known she'd better tell the truth. The Truth cost Ann's Grandfather $5000 for the attorney and $1000. for the horse. A horse that on the best sale day would be worth about $500. The Judge sentenced Ann's Mother to a year's probation with no jail time.

Ann was only 12 years old when this took place. The ranch she loved so much was repossessed by the bank when she was 16. By then she had a Driver's License, and was able to take one last drive to the ranch.

The old house was empty and the horses and cattle were gone. Ann climbed the stairs to her old room; the bed was still there. She decided to spend the night and take one last look over the valley she loved so much.

Tears kept her company as she drove away the next day. Years later she would take her children to visit this beautiful valley. There wasn't any way that they would be able to understand the sadness that was still a part of her.

Ann's Great Grandchildren also visited this valley, and they too, would never be able to understand the loss, and the pain, this elderly woman still had inside her heart.

To be young again and be able to make everything right that was wrong. To ride bareback across the hills and meadow, to watch the lightning, and to smell the fresh cut Alfalfa hay, and the Northern Lights that brightened many winter nights.

Ann has always been so thankful for these precious memories. She can bring them forth anytime she wants to take that ride, smell the fresh cut hay, watch the lightening play across the valley, or the Northern Lights display their Aura.

The Good Old Days

The Iron:

BLACKSMITHS STARTED FORGING SIMPLE FLAT irons in the late Middle Ages. Plain metal irons were heated by a fire or on a stove. ... Some irons had cool wooden handles and in 1870 a detachable handle was patented in the US. This stayed cool while the metal bases were heated and the idea was widely imitated. My Grandmother, Annie Mae DeSchamps Poloson used the Flat Iron with the detachable wooden handle. She was still using this in the early 1940's since the ranch had no electricity.

An "electric flatiron" was invented by American Henry W. Seeley and patented on June 6, 1882. It weighed almost 15 pounds and took a long time to heat.

Sarah Boone invented the ironing board in the early 1890s. She received U.S. Patent No. 473,653 on April 26, 1892 for her ironing board. Boone's board had collapsible legs so that the ironing board could be stored when it was not being used.

I always had an electric iron and an ironing board. Ironing was my least favorite household duty so when No Iron Clothing was invented I was delighted.

A chemist long affiliated with the United States Department of Agriculture, Dr. Benerito helped perfect modern wrinkle-free cotton, colloquially known as permanent press, in work that she and her colleagues began in the late 1950s. I can remember my uncle's wife's stack of clothing, that needed ironing, in her closet. I don't think she ever took them out and ironed them. Permanent Press saved the day for her too.

Washing Machines: The earliest washing "machine" was the scrub board invented in 1797. American, James King, patented the first washing machine to use a drum in 1851, the drum made King's machine resemble a modern machine, however it was still hand powered.

The Scrub Board cost $35.

30 years later, an American, Nathaniel Briggs, obtained the first patent for a washing machine. It involved pouring hot water into a tank, turning a lever to wash the clothes and then wringing them between two rollers. It was only in 1930 that the machines became automatic. Speed Queen was one of the first more modern machines. Maytag came out with a Gas model in 1927. That is what my mother used for years because we had no electricity. It was started by stepping on a pedal many times because it didn't start easily. A hose was extended to of doors so the home's occupants weren't asphyxiated.

Dryers : A Frenchman named Pochon is credited with inventing the first clothes dryer around 1800. His invention was a vented barrel hand turned over an open fire. Various adaptations were made on the dryer designs leading to the dryers we use today.

The first electric dryer was invented in the early 20th century. Inventor J. Ross Moore was tired of hanging his clothing outside, especially during the winter. To help keep his wardrobe out of the freezing weather, he built a shed to house his clothes while they dried. In addition, he added a stove. The clothing would hang on the line in front of the fire and dry. This was the beginning of the development of electric dryers. For the next three decades, Moore worked to eventually build a gas and electric unit, but couldn't find anyone to help him get his idea manufactured. The drum-type model was built and eventually picked up by Hamilton Manufacturing in Wisconsin. The new dryers were sold under the name June Day beginning in 1938.

We were never fortunate enough to have a Dryer ! Our clothes hung out and freeze dried in the winter. When my husband, Lyle was in the Navy, he had access to a dryer. That gave him the idea to buy one for his mother. That was in 1958.

I didn't have an automatic washer and a dryer until early 1970. What a blessing.

Refrigeration: The icebox was invented by an American farmer and cabinetmaker named Thomas Moore in 1802. The Ice Box required ice which was a rare commodity nine months out of the year. To get ice, you needed water to freeze, which usually meant it became winter. You stored ice in blocks from lakes in ice houses insulated with sawdust and kept the ice as cold as possible.

In the year 1805, US inventor Oliver Evans, designed the first refrigeration machine that didn't use liquid and instead used vapor to cool.

Since we didn't have electricity , we were without a refrigerator, and my parents didn't even have an Ice Box. Mom canned everything and during the summer we ate a lot of chicken. We did have a locker in Polson where we kept beef and pork. We also ate lots of eggs.

When I married and moved to the city the refrigerator had a very tiny freezer compartment. And the pesky refrigerator had to be defrosted ! Frost free refrigerators came out in the early 1950's. I didn't have one until 1962.

Freezers : The first freezers appeared during the 1940s, then known as deep freeze, it did not go into mass production until after the World War II. My Grandmother had a freezer that was located in the Cook House. I was born in 1940 so she must have purchased the freezer as soon as they were available.

Dishwashers: Josephine Garis Cochran invented the first useful dishwasher in Shelbyville, Ill., and received patent # 355,139 on December 28, 1886. Cochran, a wealthy woman who entertained often, wanted a machine that could wash dishes faster than her servants, and without breaking them.

When Miele introduced the first automated model in 1960, it was still costly – as much as a housekeeper's annual salary, in fact. Yet the concept stood the test of time and by the end of the 1970s, the dishwasher had become one of the most common home appliances." Miele and Bosch were brand names.

I had portable dishwashers starting in the mid 1960's. My first built in wasn't until we remodeled our kitchen in 1995. I have a dishwasher in the rental I live in now.

During my youth and young married life I packed wood and carried water. Hung clothes out during the winter, defrosted the refrigerator, washed clothes in an old gas powered Maytag, and didn't have the luxury of a dryer until I was 30 plus years old. The built in dishwasher when I was 55. I also washed clothes by hand for over a month; 4 children created a lot of laundry. An electric wringer washer that I purchased through the Salvation Army was a God Send.

The Good Old Days are Romantic in a good Western or Movie, but I don't care to relive those days. My Grandmother said the same and she was born in 1889. She was a Montana Homesteader so experienced the Good Old Days first hand.

Change

3 YEAR OLD GRACE GAVE NO thought to the word "change." Change began when she was 8 months old; her parents had divorced. Age 3 brought another change; a stepfather and a baby sister. The giant change arrived when she was almost 9 years old. Her stepfather left and she wasn't even told until he drove away.

Grace had no knowledge of Heraclitus, a Greek philosopher, that had been quoted as saying "change is the only constant in life." "Stability" had driven away in a 1949 Chevrolet. "Fear" went home that day.

It was getting cold with snow storms, an impassable road, and a cold house, but the real cold was inside her heart. Grace thought she'd never be warm again after her stepfather left. Snow blew in the window by her bed, and she dared not remove her clothing before climbing into the bed she shared with her sister.

When her stepfather was home, she was respected by her school mates. After he left, it was difficult riding the bus to school. Teasing and name calling were constant. She rode in the back of the old pickup; seating was on a wooden bench shared by her peers. The driver couldn't hear the mean things that were said. Grace's safe times were spent with the horses, or her grandparents, and never when she was with her peers.

The last straw happened when she was severely punished for lashing out at her sister. "No one loved her:" she would just shoot herself, and be done with all the pain of not being loved, and being scared all the time. Life was so unfair; her sister had stomped on her foot, and she wasn't punished at all.

Grace didn't realize that it took a lot of courage to fire the gun she was pointing at her head. She was a failure when it came to that kind of courage. But, she had avoided a final change. Running away was the only thing she could do. With every step, the words "reform school" played over and over in her head; if she were caught, she'd be put in reform school. She envisioned it as being like Dracula's Castle.

She arrived at a neighbors five miles from home. Maybe she would give her a job. By the time she reached Pearl's place reality was setting in. She needed a job and food. Grace was not able to think clearly at all. She was taken by surprise when Pearl reminded her that she had Grandparents ! This was wonderful because she knew they loved her. Grace's depression had created a black world where she was all alone. She had forgotten about her grandparents even though every summer had been spent with them.

She should have been happy away from her sister and the ranch, but she missed the place she'd been on for years. She missed the horses, the beautiful valley visible from her upstairs window, enhanced by the Northern Lights, and the splendid lightening storms. Grace was used to riding her horse, the 8 miles to Polson, to watch a movie. She loved the quiet as she rode home in the night. The hills, with wild life, especially the beautiful buck deer, or the chipmunk she tried to catch and failed. The fawn she fed with a bottle. She would run and play with the big Collie dog; he'd go under the fences and she'd leap over.

Memories of the best horse she had ever ridden, so smooth; so beautiful. Grace could ride him bareback as well as any Native. They were One as they moved across the land. Even memories of the 5 baby skunks. Grace had ridden several miles from the ranch house when she came upon a skunk with babies. She caught the babies and took them home. A sad memory because she'd taken that mother's babies. A change in that poor mother skunk's life, and someone got rid of the babies.

Memories of checking on the Glacier Park horses and mules during the winter. How she missed this part of her life. How could she ever leave the ranch?

It was her inability to accept, or even understand, her life changes that pulled her towards the ranch. She was an empty vessel when she was away from the place. Long after everyone was gone and the place sold, Grace would drive the rutted road to the old house. She would sleep in her room on the only bed that was left behind. It was here that she mattered.

Marriage was an escape into a make believe world she could control. But the more she tried to control the more out of control her life became. A drive to the old home place would help; she would really be; she would be important. While everything was in constant change, and usually for the worse, more trips home, and yet no peace within. Grace felt so worthless.

Grace didn't realize that the shock and trauma she felt when her stepfather left would control her life. Her emotional self was frozen; decisions, if they required feelings, were made by a 9 year old. And every mistake lead to a harsh mental beating by the grown up Grace. Feelings of inadequacy were controlling every decision, and she was scared to be alone. She replaced her stepfather with a husband she thought she could control. Her worth was zero so she picked a man worth zero; an alcoholic who cared only for alcohol and a good time.

When Grace was 42 years old a degree in Chemical Dependency Counseling, with the focus on Family, opened the door to her own healing. She was able to incorporate all the changes she had feared or abhorred as a part of who she had become. Her emotional maturity lead to a very happy marriage with a man God sent to her in a dream. She no longer drove the rutted road to the home of her childhood. She was important and she mattered.

Grace and Silvertip-Rickey

Grace & Fawn
Grace's mare, Baby Kay. Baby Kay made a 70 mile
trip carrying Grace to the home ranch.

Accident Prone

I THINK I HOLD THE RECORD for accidents. When I was 4 years old I walked across the room, in my sleep, and tumbled down the stairs. My shoulder dislocated, and when my step-father put it back in place, it was so painful.

When I was 6, I stepped on a spike. It went through my shoe, and out the top of my foot. Mom had me soak it in Epsom Salts. The problem was the wound was so deep the soaking didn't help. I ended up with blood poisoning, and spent a week in the hospital. Penicillin shots several times a day resulted in an allergic reaction. I had hives from head to toe.

My job was to bring in the milk cows so I climbed on Smoky, and went to bring them in. Smoky would shy at anything; he saw the cows laying in the tall grass, shied, and off I went. Smoky stepped on my foot; the foot that was still healing.

My cousins were visiting, and our game for the morning was running up the trunk of a tree in our bare feet. My Step-Father had just pruned the tree so sharp, short branch points were left. I slipped and as I fell, my side hung on one of those points. I had to climb up to release myself from the sharp point. This left a hole in my side that almost penetrated my lung. Mom drove me to the hospital in Polson. Surgery closed the one inch hole in my side. I still have the scar.

Our Appaloosa Stallion was blind in one eye. I was riding him when he fell, after stepping in a badger hole. I lit on my head. My speech was jumbled; shoes were called a dish, etc. Mom was going to take me to the hospital, but suddenly my speech became coherent.

After that accident and concussion, my legs became so restless. It was pure misery setting through a film at the theatre, or even setting still reading a book. This always happened in the evening. I was 12 when this accident occurred, and when I was 65 years, an ad came on the TV about restless leg. I was able to get a prescription that has given me so much relief.

My sorrel gelding, Jagade, was not very well trained. He decided to buck; off I went and dislocated my shoulder. My arm lay above my head; I had to wiggle around far enough so I could get up. My uncle was taking me to the hospital when my arm went back into place.

For years I had problems with my shoulders dislocating; a wrong move is all it would take. I had surgery on the left shoulder in 1966. Dan was a baby. I stayed with a friend until I was able to care for Dan, and my other 4 children.

We had to take our own trash to the city dump when I lived in Red Wing. A city snow plow hit a chunk of ice, and it threw the blade right into the door of my car. My head hit the rear view mirror; stitches were required. The car was a Rambler; it was totaled because of the type of frame.

Lyle and I had quite a few horses. I was riding our stallion when the bit broke; unable to control him with the mares close by, I jumped off. Chief stepped on my leg; he was shod so the injury was severe. I had to have surgery when it would not heal.

My next accident was my own stubborn fault. I had gone to get the mail while Lyle waited for me with the tractor and mower. He was upset because I hadn't gone directly to help him. When the pickup was loaded with hay, I angrily said I'd ride on top of the load. We hadn't gone far when I slid off the load and broke my pelvis. That resulted in an ambulance call, and a ride to the hospital. It was several months before I was able to walk. So much for being stubborn.

Lyle bought a big water tank he could use for a cistern to catch rain water. We buried it in the back yard and ran pipes from the eve troughs into it. Lyle was taking water from the cistern for the outdoor wood furnace. He asked me to stand on the hose to keep the end in the cistern, while he pulled the hose to the furnace. I could have stood on it 5 or 10 feet from the cistern, but I stood on the hose right on the edge of the cistern. The next thing I knew, I was in the cistern with one leg down and one leg up. It was impossible for me to do anything. Lyle had to get the neighbors to help pull me out. I had a cracked rib.

We were stacking baled hay in the barn. Lyle was operating the skid steer, and I was doing the ground work. He didn't see me and I ended up being squeezed on top of a bale. Thankfully, the only thing that was hurt was my pride. I quit and went to the house.

I was taking a swatch of mane from our palomino mare for a DNA test. Lyle raised a switch to move the other horses along; the palomino jumped and my shoulder went out of place. The ER again.

My right shoulder went out again when I reached up to hug a friend. Back to the ER. I had surgeries on both shoulders to correct this. They were performed in different years. After Lyle passed away, Becky and Bernie came for his funeral, and to help me. Becky and I were feeding Fawn and a blue roan mare we were boarding. The blue roan ran up behind me, passed, and kicked with both hind feet. She hit my mouth resulting in stitches on my upper lip. I swallowed so much Novcane as the doctor gave me shots to numb the pain. Dr. Anderson prided himself in his beautiful stitching. True to his word, my scar is almost invisible.

My age and lack of balance lead to more accidents after I moved to Kalispell. I tripped going into Rosaur's, and fell. Two men came to my rescue. I was bruised and sore but nothing was broken.

Parking too close to the curb resulted in my tripping over the curb. I managed to crawl far enough to grab the door handle so I could pull myself up. This was in front of Costco.

I enrolled in balance classes at the Summit. During the icy weather I wore cleats. For several years I was accident free.

Easter of 2021, I drove to Spokane to spend time with Dan's widow and my grandchildren. On Easter Sunday I tripped over a raise in the sidewalk and skinned my arm. My skin is so thin it bled profusely. Rhett, my grandson, helped me up, and bandaged my arm. I didn't get blood on my nice blouse. That was my main concern.

In late August 2021, I drove to Spokane to visit. This time Harley, my grandchildren's dog, jumped up and dug his claws into my arm; it was accidental. Rhett and Jill, my daughter in law, wrapped and bandaged my arm.

I have had a lot of experience with "thin skin". I bumped the railing going into my grandchildren's home; this also required a bandaid.

When I meet my Maker, it will probably be by accident!

My Diverse Occupations

FROM AGE 3 TO 16 farm and ranch chores caring for the chickens, cows, and horses. I carried water, and cut & packed wood for the fire in the heater and cookstove. When I was 13, I cut Christmas Trees to earn money. When I was 14-15-16 feeding my Grandfather's 2000 head of sheep, harnessing the team, starting the D-4 Cat, and chopping hay for the sheep.

Age 16- Married Leo. We were married in Coeur d'Alene, Idaho. I had never seen a roller coaster and had no idea what it was! Leo bought tickets, and I was on the scariest ride of my life. I was wishing I could just die and get it over with. He thought it was funny. We met in Whitefish, and as soon as we were married moved to Red Wing, Minnesota.

Leo was out of work so we moved to Colbran, Colorado where my Mother lived. My son, Kevin Leo was born July 22, 1958. I was 18 that following November 22nd. Leo worked for Dr. Ziegel to pay the doctor and hospital bills; a total of $190.

Then back to Minnesota, and to the Twin Cities. I worked for Old Dutch Potato Chips packing bags of potato chips in boxes. I worked at White Castle for a while; an incident caused me to quit. There wasn't any bus service after Midnight when I got off work. It was 30 blocks home, but I had no choice but to walk. A car started following me; he went around the block several times. I made it to a phone booth and called Leo at work; he came and drove me home.

Age 19–A Nursing home as cook for 44 residents and also patient care. This was for Daley's Rest Home in Red Wing, Minnesota. I was pregnant with my second son, Keith Galen. We stayed with

Leo's parents until after Keith was born April 21, 1960. Then we moved back to the Cities again. Leo was working for the Rock Island Railroad so I was a stay at home Mom for a while.

Age 21- I went to work for Lawrence Laundry. In the morning I put eye glass towels through a huge mangel. There were 2 women who worked with me. In the afternoon, I worked alone. My job was putting continuous towels through the same mangel. I put 2000 continuous towels through that mangle every afternoon. I worked at that laundry for 2.5 years.

Age 23- I was pregnant with my daughter, Rene Janine. We had moved to Ellsworth, Wisconsin. Leo was drawing unemployment. Rene was born March 25,1963. We moved back to the Twin Cities again. I went to work for Frito Lay Potato Chips packing small packets into boxes for shipping.

Age 24-Various jobs cleaning houses, etc.

Age 24-My daughter, Robin Bach, was born October 2, 1964 at the Plum City Wisconsin hospital. We were living in a farm house near there.

Age 25-June 5, 1965 I married Vernon.

Age 26-June 5, 1966, my son, Dan, was born in Red Wing, MN.

AGE-26-Worked at the Cherry Hump factory in Winona, MN. (This company went out of business in 1987.

Age 27-29-Learned how to paint homes and buildings. Vern was a painter by trade, so I learned from him. I was more particular, and worked with him to assure a job well done.

Age 29-1969 Owner-Operator of Day Care employed 3 women, and I also drove Taxi in the afternoon when the children were napping.

Age 31 to Age 40-Journeyman Painter–Joined the Painter's Union. Painted homes in Red Wing, Minnesota and Nybo's huge dining room.

Painted Country Kitchen and Pizza Hut in Missoula, an apartment building, and many houses. I also painted the gates on Kerr Dam.

Age 33-Summer of 1973- Ran a Pettybone Rubber Tired Skidder and skidded logs. I was able to skid 200 logs a day.

Age 34 to 37-Was hired by Endresse Painting, then the Anaconda Company at their new Arbitor Plant.

Age 37-The Arbiter Plant closed. Went to work for a Paint Contractor in Butte; became his Foreman. Painted homes, Montana Power Buildings, etc. When his work was finished I went work for an outfit out of Texas. My boss wore a cowboy hat. I painted pipes, etc. the same as I'd done at the Arbitor Plant. This identified the chemicals that ran through the pipes. I sandblasted the Combustion Pit for the MHD Plant. I think the plan, that never came to be, was to turn coal into gas.

Age 39-Went to work at the Montana State Prison as the Inmate Paint Crew Supervisor. I had 11 inmates on my crew. We painted the new cubes and bunks for the new prison buildings, and also outlying ranch buildings.

Was called back by the Anaconda Company. They paid $3 an hour more than the State paid at the prison. I stayed with the company until they closed down in 1980. Chili had seized the Copper Processing Plant in that country, and this caused the Anaconda Company to go out of business.

1980–Age 40-43 Spokane Falls Community College Substance Abuse Course and also a Writing Class. Almut McAuley was my writing instructor. That is when I wrote The Making Of A Con, the sad story about Grant Hamilton's life in and out of prisons.

Age 43- Graduated with Honors. I had one B and all the rest of my grades were A's. I was so thankful. I had completed the 8th grade when I was 12. My High School Correspondence Course was paid for by my Grandmother, and as stated previously, I took mainly Agriculture classes. I did receive a Diploma. That and my life experiences allowed admission to Spokane Falls Community College.

CD & Family Counselor Colstrip and Forsyth, Montana. My job covered Rosebud and Treasure Counties. I worked from Colstrip for 2 years then took over the Forsyth Office. I traveled to see clients in Ashland, Lame Deer, and Hysham. One community each week.

During these years, I attended so many Seminars; the ones that interested me the most, and were the most beneficial to my clients were the Adult Children Of Alcoholic Seminars. I was able to start support groups, and the clients I worked with have remained sober and have stable families.

Age 46-Robin passed away February 19th. The pain that I felt was so deep. Robin had Progressive Multiple Sclerosis. She was diagnosed at 26 and passed when she was 41.

Age 66-73- Lyle retired January 1, 2001. I was so glad to have him home every day. We could do things together. Lyle raised a huge garden and planted Apple Trees. We made Apple Cider and canned so many vegetables and fruits. We raised and sold horses. 2 sales we are so proud of; a palomino mare went to Israel, and a black mare was sold to the Netherlands. I started writing again during this time. An Immigrant A Homesteader And Sheep was started in 2012.

Our Travels: We went to the San Diego Zoo, Sea World, Yosemite, The Grand Canyon, Jackson Hole, Teddy Roosevelt's Badlands in North Dakota, the Pryor Wild Horse Range, Glacier Park, and Yellowstone Park, Craters Of The Moon in Idaho, the Petrifie Rock Park in Lemmon, SD. Our favorite, horseback camping trips in the Big Horn Mountains.

Age 73- Lyle passed away December 16, 2013. I stayed on our place until November of 2014 when I moved to Kalispell. Lyle had kept up the yard, garden, apple trees, and any maintenance on the buildings. I am accident prone so made the decision to sell the place.

Age 74-79-I joined the Kalispell Senior Center. I found all the letters Lyle had saved during our courtship. That prompted the book "Once In A Lifetime Comes A Man." I finished "An Immigrant A Homesteader And Sheep."

My main focus during this time was Aunt Fay Poloson Haynes. She was 88 years old. Macular Degeneration had become so advanced she could no longer drive. I would drive to her place near Ronan, and we would take trips to Hot Springs, going past her and Bill's Big Bend Ranch. The Pizza Hut in Polson was one of her favorites or the restaurant in Ronan's Cheeseburgers. Fay enjoyed coffee time and rodeos. We went to lots of rodeos and watched them on her television too. And we took trips to Glacier Park. One trip was special because her sister-in-law, Grace, was able to get a leave from the rest home and go with us.

July 21, 2019 My son, Dan, passed away in Sacramento, California. My son, Kevin, and I drove to the Funeral which was in Dixon, California. Dan was laid to rest in the Dixon Military Cemetery. His widow, Jill, and their children, Rhett, Savannah, and Ginny were there. We didn't have a lot of time to visit since Kevin had to be back to work.

Aunt Fay passed away on November 22, 2019, my 79th birthday. She didn't have anything prepared, and only a few of the pallbearers she had listed were still alive. So this was another funeral I had to plan; I'd planned Robin's and Lyle's although he let me know what he wanted. Fay was a month short of her 94th birthday. A life so well lived.

Age 79 to Present I completed "Once In A Lifetime Comes A Man", pulled "The Making Of A Con" out of the drawer and published it, published "An Immigrant A Homesteader And Sheep", "Bum Lambs", "Fay", and "Montana's Last Hanging."

This is my 8th book now. It is made up of short stories, and I have no idea what to name it.

Age 80-Made a trip to Spokane to visit Grandchildren then a trip to Minnesota to visit my daughter, Rene, her husband, Steve, and my 6 Great Grandchildren.

Made a trip to Spokane again in late August. The name for my short story book was my Granddaughter, Gin's, brilliant mind. "Dusk Till Dawn In The Wild World." Very fitting as the stories are so different; some true and some fiction.

Spring On The Poloson Ranch

MEMORIES HAVE ARRIVED WITH SPRING. I live in the city now but I miss the country life, and all that went with it.

I walk out of the Great Room where Aunt Fay's paintings grace the walls, A Navajo rug covers the back of the sofa. The old record player is by the fireplace. The Cowboy Clock and the Bucking Horse Lamp decorate the end tables. I pass the spacious kitchen and dining areas as I walk to the front door.

As I scan the valley below, all Poloson Ranch owned, my favorite memory is the wonderful smell of Sagebrush. The familiar smell made me feel alive, grounded, and a part of nature. Sagebrush is Native to the land below the ranch house.

As my Grandmother steps from her house, she passes the giant heirloom Yellow Rose she planted in 1930. The Chickadees she fed all winter have returned to the forest. The Robins, and Blue and Gray Jays have returned.

I can see my Grandmother, with her hoe, opening the small ditches to the trees behind her house. Once this is done, Grandma walks a mile to the Big Orchard ; she is clearing the irrigation ditch as she moves along the path. Apple, Plum, Cherry, and Pear Trees are flourishing because of my Grandmother's care. Grandma always walked by the spring where Watercress grew. We enjoyed Watercress Salad every Spring and Summer. My Grandmother walked with a cane because of an accident years ago.

The grass is several inches high, and the field below the house will soon be pastured; the milk cow and saddle horses are kept in that field because it is close to the barn and corrals. Calving will begin soon. I remember helping my Grandfather pull a calf when a heifer was unable to calve on her own.

100 head of cattle and 2000 head of sheep supported the ranch. I can still hear, in memory, the bleat of the ewes calling their lambs. I'm harnessing the team so Grandpa and I can feed the sheep and cattle. We hauled the hay on a rubber tired wagon. The hay for the ewes had to be chopped so I start up the D-4 Cat and we chopped alfalfa hay; there is no waste with chopped hay.

When the lambing is done it is shearing time. The Shearers come from Washington, and the same family has been shearing Grandpa's sheep for years. Next comes dipping for ticks. A deep cement trough is filled with a creosote mixture. The ewes are pushed into this, swim through, then climb up the ramp. It has taken a very long day.

The lamb's tails are docked; this prevents infections. All of the buck lambs are castrated. My Grandfather does this with his teeth; again to prevent infection. Grandpa was from Romania, and this method was passed down through many generations.

Soon, the sheep will be on pasture, and the end of May, on their way to the St. Joe National Forest in Idaho. The pack horses are shod and will be hauled to St Regis. That is where the sheep will be herded up the mountain and into Idaho. Grandpa trailed the sheep from the ranch to St. Regis with his dogs and saddle horse. His tent and supplies followed in the old International Pickup. I always thought it as tough as a military tank.

The dining room and kitchen are quiet. Life slows for my Aunt Betty; she prepared all the meals for the crews from December through Mid May. Uncle Bert, their 2 children, and I now share Betty's wonderful meals. My Grandmother has her own home; a rock path leads from the ranch house to her small, wood framed home. It was built when Homesteading opened on the Flathead Indian Reservation in 1910, so it is almost 50 years old. Wood floors, no running water, or indoor bathroom.

Grandma's home was my haven. She had a round library table covered with magazines; Colliers, National Geographic, Saturday Evening Post, Holiday, and Readers' Digest. An Indian Tomahawk sat on this table; it is now in the Miracle Of America Museum, Polson, Montana.

My Grandmother was a wonderful cook. She would make head cheese for Grandpa, and grind horseradish, which he loved. No one could ever cook eggs like my Grandmother. And no one in our family could eat hot peppers and horseradish like my Grandfather. Not even a tear!

I am so thankful for my Memories. What a precious gift from God.

Uncle Fred Poloson standing on the porch of the new Poloson ranch house in 1948

The Poloson Ranch

Dusk Till Dawn in the Wild World

This is in Memory of my daughter, Robin, and my son, Dan. They were teenagers when this took place.

Impatience

Robin said, "Let's go, Mom."

"Wait a minute. I have to take the rollers out of my hair."

"Come on, Mom, we have to bowl in fifteen minutes."

"Robin, I asked you if you were going to bowl two days ago, and you said no. I wish you would have told me. I have to meet Midge for coffee too. I guess I can drop you off on the way."

"Mom, hurry up or we will be late."

"Robin, do you want me to take Red home after you are done bowling?"

"No, she is going to stay overnight at our place."

"Thank God, the gas tank is getting low and it has to last until Friday. Is Danny going to bowl too?"

"If he ever gets ready to go or we will leave him. Come on Danny, you are always late. I am not loaning you money either. Come on, Mom you look okay. Now, hurry up. I'm going to go back the car out of the garage right now."

"Robin, be careful, don't hit the house and watch out for the cat; Dan tried to catch him but he got out."

"Oh, Mom, I know how to drive and I have backed the car out of the garage 100s of times."

"Well, we can't afford to be fixing the car or the Landlord's house, and I ran over Kevin's cat when he was only four years old. That was awful.".

"Mom, Kevin is 24 years old now, and I'm not going to hit the house or run over the cat."

"Okay, I'll be there as soon as I shut the lights off."

"See, Mom, I backed out okay. You were looking out the window weren't you? Bet you thought I'd hit the house. I told you."

Some Quotes On Aging:

It is the body that ages, but the mind remains forever young. This is why we fall and break something as we dash down the steps, or across the lawn, or try to head off that Grandchild before he falls. Our mind seems stuck at 16 and it never catches up with the age of our body.

We didn't get old on purpose, it just happened. If you're lucky, it could happen to you. – Andy Rooney I can remember when my sister and I thought anyone over 50 was ancient, and we would never be 50; we'd be forever young. But age sneaked up on us and now we are looking back 26 and 29 years to that ancient age of 50.

The cardiologist's diet: If it tastes good spit it out. – Anonymous I made Reuben Sandwiches for my husband and I years ago using fat free cheese. We were not able to eat the tasteless sandwiches and our dog turned his nose up.

My 95 year old friend, Rosie, said she asked one of the Darigold stockers "how can they make "fat free" sour cream." He said, "It sounds incredible."

The old begin to complain of the conduct of the young when they themselves are no longer able to set a bad example. – François de la Rochefoucauld

I find myself judging the way some young people dress or act, and some of the words we never would have used are standard now. The movies that are famous today can never replace "Gone With The Wind." And the Hollywood heart throbs don't hold a candle to Clark Gable, John Wayne, Kirk Douglas, and Robert Mitchum, and so many others both men and women. Susan Hayward, Lucille Ball, and Rita Hayworth. And the all time comedies of Carol Burnett.

I just read an article on the Movie Stars of old in comparison to those of today. Every single actor and some of the actresses were in the Military. Some were Gunners; some were Pilots; some were Nurses. Men and women who kept this country free. I could not find one movie actor or actress that is in Hollywood today that has been in the military. Maybe that is why I seldom watch a movie. The last one I went to was "Racing In The Rain." I was not familiar with the actors and the actress but it was an excellent movie, although sad in places.

As an artist with Hallmark™ since 1970, John Wagner created Maxine 36 years ago in 1986. Maxine gives us a reason to smile, and frequently to laugh out loud.

Search this webs Humorous quotes about aging bring forth the finer nuances of growing up and aging. They help you see the lighter side of life and make you love it even more "Age is an issue of mind over matter. If you don't mind, it doesn't matter." — Mark Twain.

Why isn't the number 11 pronounced oneity-one?

If a pig loses its voice is it called disgruntled ?

The 8 Decades I Have Lived

1940's

Gone With The Wind was playing at theaters throughout the United States. The film was adapted from the 1936 novel by Margaret Mitchell.

Franklin D. Roosevelt was elected President for a third term 2 weeks before I was born, November 22, 1940.

The Holocaust was happening in Germany, but few knew the Jewish people were being put to death by Hitler. My Step Father always used the word "Jew" whenever he thought the person had cheated him. Maybe listening to Hitler's media continually hating the Jewish people? Could that have affected my Step Father's beliefs? Or was it because the Jewish were bankers, and they were blamed for the Depression? He didn't know that 5000 Jews were confined in ghettos, and that they had to wear the "mark", a star which identified them. And he had no idea that Hitler was gassing 1000's of Jewish people every day, and no one was allowing that truth to hit the radio air waves. There is the question of where all the money went when the banks closed in "dirty '30's." The Rothschild's and the Rockefeller's remained very wealthy while millions lost everything.

Move forward to the 2000's : An oil industry insider with House of Saud connections, wrote in The Grim Reaper that information he acquired from Saudi bankers cited 80% ownership of the New York Federal Reserve Bank- by far the most powerful Fed branch- by just eight families, four of which reside in the US. They are the Goldman Sachs, Rockefellers', Lehmans and Kuhn Loebs of New York.

The Japanese attacked the US base at Pearl Harbor on Sunday, December 7,1941. I was a Year old. Our ships were bombed leaving close to 2500 of the Navy's young men dead, and over a 1000 injured. President Roosevelt stated that December 7, 1941 was a day of Infamy. War was declared against Japan.

World War II in Europe began when Hitler's Nazi Germany attacked Poland. Germany had allies such as Italy, Hungary, Bulgaria, and Romania. These European countries were part of the Axis of Powers. The two main causes of the World War II were the rise of militaristic totalitarian regimes in Germany, Japan and Italy mainly due to the great depression of the 1930's, and the Treaty of Versailles conditions following World War I, and the inability and failure of the League Of Nations to deals with various International Issues.

U.S. Combat Dead in Europe-Atlantic 183,588 Army ground forces, of these, 141,088 Army, Air Force 36,461, and Navy/Coast Guard 6,039. The Asia–Pacific,108,504 Army ground forces of which 41,592 were Army, Air Force 15,694, Navy/Coast Guard, 31,485, Marine Corp, 19,733. So, we as a country, lost 292,092 men and women in WW II. The United States was made up of 48 states so the WW II deaths would have been 6,085.25 men and women from each state, just to give readers an idea of how devastating the war was. This isn't even taking into consideration the 1000's of wounded, many who never recovered enough to even enjoy their lives., or the Prisoners Of War. Very Sad.

World War II casualties–Wikipedia

During World War II farmers had to make do with the tires and machinery they had. All the rubber and metals went to the war effort. Machines were held together with "baling wire." Tires were repaired and used until they were totally thread bare. Groceries were rationed and everyone was given ration stamps.

My Mom and Step Father raised chickens. They had a Brooder House where they raised the baby chickens they had ordered through the mail. These were picked up at the Post Office. We also had 2 milk cows. Eggs and cream were traded for groceries. We ate a lot of fried chicken in the summer, and we did have pigs and beef cattle. Beef and pork were winter food except for the meat we stored in a rented locker at the Locker Plant in Polson. Shoes had to last; one pair a year. I have crooked toes and Uncle Fred did too. He had to have a toe removed because it was so crooked. Our feet grew but the shoe size remained the same.

My Grandparents had a sheep ranch, 2000 head. There were so many homeless men; older men that needed a place to stay and work for room and board. The war had kept people working, and when it was over the weapons factories and ship building yards shut down. 1000's were released from the military.

I remember we were all poor but everyone was happy that the war was finally over. We had been fighting in Europe as well as the Pacific. So many died in battle, and others came home suffering from injuries and Post Traumatic Stress.

The pickups that we had were gas; our tractors too. We used Kerosene in the washing machine engine. White gas was used for our lantern that hung from a hook in the ceiling. Our clothes were washed, put through a wringer into the rinse tub then put through the wringer again, and hung on the clothesline to dry. Our clothes freeze dried in the winter. We had clothes racks or a line across the room to thaw them, and finish their drying.

Bathing was done in a wash tub approximately 2.5 feet across; a round tub about 18 inches deep. Us kids didn't look forward to our weekly bath. We had stock ponds to play in but they weren't that clean. My description of myself was "Ragamuffin."

I went to school in the one room Big Arm School. Maggie Lannon was my 1st and 2nd grade teacher. J.B. Kircoff was County Superintendent. He always spent extra time with me when he came to the school. Mrs. Mueller taught the 3rd and 4th grade. I started school at 5 years then took the 3rd and 4th grade together, so I was out of school at age 12 when I completed the 8th grade. High School was a Correspondence Course Grandma Mae bought for me.

1947 : Chuck Yeager broke the sound barrier with his plane.

1949 : the United States joined NATO, the National Atlantic Treat Organization.

1950's

The Korean War began in 1952. Harry Truman was President ; he replaced Roosevelt when he passed. Truman was his Vice President. I remember Truman fired General Douglas MacArthur.

I was so angry. MacArthur was my hero. Our military fought in freezing weather without warm clothing. They were poorly prepared for the rugged mountains, freezing temperatures, and the cunning enemy. The war ended with the 38th Parallel being agreed upon separating North Korea from South Korea. The Korean Armistice Agreement brought an end to the hostilities that killed 2.5 million people on July 27, 1953, that ceasefire never gave way to a peace treaty. At the time, South Korea's president refused to accept the division of Korea.

US and South Korean prisoners of war were paraded through the streets of Pyongyang by communist troops during the Korean War. A United States officer was forced to wear a Hitler mustache and swastikas and drag a US flag.

The Korean War was a military and diplomatic disaster from its very beginning. After North Korean forces invaded South Korea in June 1950, the United States led United Nations forces to defend South Korea. North Korea was advised, armed and trained by the USSR, and China came to its aid with over 2 million soldiers—the first time the Chinese military had fought on a large scale outside of China.

For two years, both sides fought around the 38th parallel, achieving a complete stalemate that was matched by a stalemate at the negotiating table between the parties, who could not agree on how to cease the war. Nearly 37,000 Americans were killed during the war. At least 1 million South Korean civilians were killed, and 7,000 South Korean military members died. In North Korea, 406,000 soldiers died, and 600,000 civilians were killed. Another 600,000 Chinese military members died in the war, too. And then there were the POWs who were not returned at all.

The Korean War news that we received came to our house through a battery operated radio.

I never saw a television until the black and white TV at my Grandparent's. Gunsmoke was my uncle's favorite, and my aunt liked Alfred Hitchcock. Records were popular and almost everyone had a phonograph. Buddy Holly and Elvis Presley overshadowed Tex Ritter, Ernest Tubb, and others. Johnny Cash, Faron Young, and Waylon Jennings were new on the scene. The Everly Brothers came out with "By By Love."

Jerry Lee Lewis became famous for his piano music. "Crazy Arms" sold 300,000 copies in the South, but it was his 1957 hit "Whole Lotta Shakin' Goin' On" that shot Lewis to fame worldwide. He followed this with the major hit "Great Balls of Fire."

Movies were a family affair. Westerns, Romance, and War shows came to the small theaters in Hot Springs and Polson, Montana. "Gone With The Wind",was playing again. The movie of all time came out in the late '30's. Clark Gable was my heart throb after I outgrew Audie Murphy. I used to ride my horse, 8 miles, to the movies in Polson. Then 8 miles home. I would tie the horse behind the theatre.

Families would have friends and neighbors over for cards and dinners. When it was haying and harvesting time the neighbors would help each other. Women would prepare huge, tasty meals; and a meal wasn't a meal without pie. Grandpa and Grandma had a cook for the sheep ranch employees. The Cookhouse table was 12 feet long with wooden benches for seating. A wood cookstove was used to prepare all of the meals. The cooks were usually transient and stayed for a season or so then moved on.

Cattle, sheep, and wool were finally bringing fair prices. Grandpa bought a new Chevrolet car; a Bel Air. It was beautiful. He kept his old International Pickup and the 2 ton truck; both 1947 models. I always thought that pickup was built like a tank; it was solid steel and Grandpa drove it over hill and dale where the faint hearted got out and walked.

Kevin was born July 22, 1958 in Collbran, Colorado. Doctor Ziegel owned the hospital and clinic, and a large ranch. His fee for delivering Kevin was $65. and the hospital bill was $125.

My husband then, Leo Bach, paid both bills by working in the hay fields for Dr. Ziegel.

The 1959 Hebgen Lake earthquake also known as the 1959 Yellowstone earthquake occurred on August 17th. The earthquake measured 7.2 on the Moment Magnitude scale, and caused a huge landslide resulting in 28 fatalities. My first born son was a year old. We were living in Minneapolis. I could not believe it at first. I was so sad for those who had lost loved ones.

General Dwight D. Eisenhower was elected President. He was responsible for the Freeways that made travel so much safer. The idea was a plane could land on the freeway, anywhere in the country, if we were at war. That never came about and the America of the 21st Century could not survive without the freeways. Eisenhower also warned abut the "Military-Industrial Complex."

He didn't want war, and didn't want companies making money off of wars. Eisenhower is the General who took his troops into Germany to free the Jewish people. He also made the Media photograph and help bury the dead, and the reason was the Media had been covering up what Hitler was doing. General Eisenhower wanted those so called journalists to see exactly what they had hidden from the world, the Holocaust!

1960's

I gave birth to 4 more children: Keith Galen April 21, 1960, Rene Janine March 25, 1963, Robin Rae October 2, 1964, and Dan June 5, 1966. Dan was named after Grandpa Dan Poloson.

The Beatles were popular. Frank Sinatra's "I Did It My Way" was one of the songs Elvis sang. It was debatable who was the most popular, Elvis or the Beatles. The Rolling Stones, and The Who were also popular. Simon & Garfunkel sang "The Sound Of Silence," "Mrs. Robinson" (1968), "The Boxer" (1969), and "Bridge over Troubled Water" (1970)—reached number one on singles charts worldwide. I loved their music.

Free thinking, open sexuality, and femininity changed the country. Grandparents didn't recognize the 60's generation. Birth control came upon the scene, and women could be free lovers without worry, and parents could plan their families. I remember this being a Godsend for me as well as my women friends.

Then our beloved President John F. Kennedy was assassinated November 22, 1963 on my 23rd birthday. People were in shock; how could our President be dead? Murdered? The radio news programs and the newspapers were filled with conspiracy theories. Finally, they said Lee Harvey Oswald killed the President. Case closed except it was never really closed. Throughout the years different versions of his killing have been discussed with no real answers.

JFK was in favor of an intervention in Viet Nam to stop Communism. He would not live to see the resulting war.

LBJ, Lyndon Baynes Johnson, became President since he was JFK's Vice President. For a decade that claimed to be all about peace, the Sixties were remarkably violent. In America, President Kennedy was assassinated, followed by his brother, Robert who was shot on Dan's 2nd birthday, and died early on the 6th of June 1968. Reverend Martin Luther King Jr. was shot. The Viet Nam War erupted in Southeast Asia. Violence begat violence on campuses all around the world. And the youth started making their voices heard.

But there was much more to Sixties history than violence. In fact, the refrain "Make Love, Not War," was the true chant of the younger generation, led by emerging rock bands like The Beatles, The Rolling Stones, and The Who.

Johnson's pledge to alleviate poverty saw him initiating food stamps, Medicare, Medicaid, Work Study, and Head Start among various other programs. He did manage to make an impact on poverty during his six years in office.

By 1967, the protest against U.S. participation in the Vietnam War had grown stronger, as growing numbers of Americans questioned whether the U.S. war effort could succeed, or was morally justifiable. They took their protests to the streets in peace marches, demonstrations, and acts of civil disobedience.

The U.S. Congress passed the Gulf of Tonkin Resolution and gave President Lyndon B. Johnson broad authority to increase American military presence in Vietnam. Johnson ordered the deployment of combat units for the first time and increased troop levels to 184,000.

The war exacted an enormous human cost: estimates of the number of Vietnamese soldiers and civilians killed range from 966,000 to 3 million. Some 275,000–310,000 Cambodians, 20,000–62,000 Laotians, and 58,220 U.S. service members died in the conflict, and 1,626 remain missing in action.

On November 5, 1968, American voters elected Richard Milhous Nixon as the thirty-seventh president of the United States.

Nixon Prolonged the Vietnam War for Political Gain. Nixon ran on a platform that opposed the Vietnam war, but to win the election, he needed the war to continue.

In 1968, the Paris Peace talks, intended to put an end to the 13-year-long Vietnam War, failed because an aide working for then-Presidential candidate Richard Nixon convinced the South Vietnamese to walk away from the dealings, says a new report by the BBC's David Taylor. By the late 1960s Americans had been involved in the Vietnam War for nearly a decade, and the ongoing conflict was an incredibly contentious issue.

Nixon's Presidential campaign needed the war to continue, since Nixon was running on a platform that opposed the war. Nixon feared a breakthrough at the Paris Peace talks designed to find a negotiated settlement to the Vietnam war, and he knew this would derail his campaign. In late October 1968, there were major concessions from Hanoi which promised to allow meaningful talks to get underway in Paris, concessions that would justify Johnson calling for a complete bombing halt of North Vietnam. This was exactly what Nixon feared.

Eventually, Nixon won by just 1 percent of the popular vote. "Once in office he escalated the war into Laos and Cambodia, with the loss of an additional 22,000 American lives, before finally settling for a peace agreement in 1973 that was within grasp in 1968," says the BBC.

1970's

The Viet Nam War : North Vietnam was supported by the Soviet Union, China, and other communist allies; South Vietnam was supported by the United States, South Korea, the Philippines,

Australia, Thailand, and other anti-communist allies. The war, considered a Cold War-era proxy war by some lasted almost 20 years with direct U.S. involvement ending in 1973.

I remember the people being against our Military and blaming them for the war. I had purchased a Day Care Center, and was living in Red Wing, Minnesota. I had heated arguments as I stood up for our Veterans returning from that war. My arguments; we never should have gone there, and these Soldiers and Marines were Drafted. They didn't have a choice unless they moved to Canada.

The Elite managed to keep their sons out of the war; a meeting was arranged for Bill Clinton with Col. William A. Hawkins. Hawkins was the only man in the State of Arkansas who could rescind the induction notice. Clinton's induction notice was rescinded and he was admitted into the Arkansas University R.O.T.C. program, after he promised to enroll in law school at the University of Arkansas. Bill's new draft classification was 1-D (ROTC deferment). For the remainder of the summer, Bill Clinton went to Washington D.C. and worked with the anti-war movement.

In 1972, Jane Fonda made a trip to North Vietnam where she broadcast 10 radio shows that denounced the U.S. government and military leaders. Fonda's trip became the subject of controversy when a photo surfaced of Fonda sitting in an anti-aircraft battery in Hanoi. Fonda apologized for the incident in a 1988 interview with Barbara Walters, saying, "I will go to my grave regretting the photograph of me in an anti-aircraft gun, which looks like I was trying to shoot at American planes. It hurt so many soldiers. It galvanized such hostility. It was the most horrible thing I could possibly have done. It was just thoughtless." Despite frequent bad press, Fonda continues to insist her actions were always in protest of the U.S. government and not soldiers.

I will not watch films starring Jane Fonda. She may have apologized but her actions were a show of hostility against our Military men and women. She joined the anti soldier movement along with Clinton and so many others. The younger generation had no idea the young men had been drafted and didn't have a choice. Our military was treated with horrible disrespect. It has taken years for that to change.

Now we have the Memorial and the Viet Nam Wall. A Replica of that Wall is shown in various communities. I was blessed with being able to visit the Wall when it came to Kalispell. I found the photo of Mike Smith who was killed in Viet Nam. When he was a small boy, his mother would bring him to the Poloson Ranch. I have a photo of Mike and our pet deer. It still breaks my heart over his death and the 1000's of others who had no choice.

On August 8, 1974, President Richard M. Nixon announces his intention to become the first president in American history to resign. With impeachment proceedings underway against him for his involvement in the Watergate affair, Nixon was finally bowing to pressure from the public and Congress to leave the White House. VP Gerald Ford became President. He eventually pardoned President Nixon.

New Right conservatives resented and resisted what they saw as government meddling. For example, they fought against high taxes, environmental regulations, highway speed limits, national park policies in the West (the so-called "Sagebrush Rebellion") and affirmative action and school desegregation plans. The first seat belt law was a federal law, Title 49 of the United States Code, Chapter 301, Motor Safety Standard, which took effect on January 1, 1968, that required all vehicles (except buses) to be fitted with seat belts in all designated seating positions. It didn't become compulsory until 1991.

Nuclear Power was considered dangerous after the meltdown at Three Mile Island in Pennsylvania.

People thought we had an endless supply of gasoline. These assumptions were demolished in 1973, when an oil embargo imposed by members of the Organization of Arab Petroleum Exporting Countries (OAPEC) led to fuel shortages and sky-high prices throughout much of the decade.

Gas shortages occurred along with signs, "Ask Nixon for some." In June of 1973, the price of a gallon of gasoline was under 50 cents. By May of 1974, it had skyrocketed to over $4.00 per gallon. The shortage and price hike were reportedly due to two major oil refineries being closed. Supply couldn't keep up with demand and everyone was scrambling to get the gas they needed; mainly so they could get to work. Vehicles of the 1970's were gas guzzlers, so a tank of gas didn't last long. It got so bad that people were regularly syphoning gas from unattended vehicles. Vehicles waiting for gas stretched for hundreds of yards. Service stations limited the number of gallons a person could buy. "Out Of Gas" signs were everywhere.

During the worst of the gas shortages, I was working construction, as a Journeyman Painter, and had a 5 mile drive to work. In 1976, when I was hired by the Anaconda Company, I was the 1st woman hired by them in the Trades.

Deer Lodge County, of which Anaconda was the County Seat, had a Poor Farm. It was located a few miles from Anaconda. The folks cared for chickens, a garden, and a milk cow. I would stop and visit with one of the older men that lived there. He was content and enjoyed caring for the garden, chickens, and the milk cow. Sadly, the poor farm was shut down. This farm was unique as most were not the best place for the poor. Many were work houses without pay. The Anaconda Poor House closed down in 1975.

August 16, 1977, Elvis Presley died ! What a shock to my co-workers and me. We were listening to the radio in the carpenter shop during lunch. The sadness lasted for weeks, and everyone was searching for their Elvis Records.

James Earl Carter Jr. (born October 1, 1924) was elected the 39th president of the United States from 1977 to 1981. He was a peanut farmer by trade but held many public offices including Governor of Georgia. Carter pardoned the Viet Nam War draft dodgers. He established the Departments of Energy & Education.

1980's

Carter lost to President Ronald Reagan in the 1980 election. Reagan scored a decisive 489-49 victory in the Electoral College. Republicans gained control of the Senate for the first time since 1955 by winning 12 seats. At that time there was no such thing as Red and Blue states.

The Anaconda Company shut down due to a massive loss when Chile took over their mining and smelters. I was laid off so decided to attend college in Spokane. That meant selling the home I had so lovingly remodeled. But college was opening new doors for me. One of my studies besides Substance Abuse was a Writing class with Almut McCauley. "The Making Of A Con" was written during that time.

Lyle Larson & I were married December 30, 1982. He was a staunch Conservative and Reagan supporter, and I was a Painter's Union Democrat. I would argue with Lyle, but finally realized that he had the right ideas. As I write this, I look back on Reagan as one of our Great Presidents. I graduated from Spokane Falls Community College with a degree in Substance Abuse Counseling, June of 1983, and I, who had been out of school at age 12, and finished a correspondence HS Course, mainly agriculture studies, graduated with Honors. One B and all the rest A's.

President Reagan served from 1981 until 1989. "Reaganomics", advocated tax rate reductions to spur economic growth, economic deregulation, and reduction in government spending. In his first term, he survived an assassination attempt, spurred the War on Drugs, invaded Grenada, and fought public sector labor unions.

Over his two terms, the economy saw a reduction of inflation from 12.5% to 4.4% and an average real GDP annual growth of 3.6%. Reagan enacted cuts in domestic discretionary spending, cut taxes, and increased military spending, which contributed to increased federal debt overall. Foreign affairs dominated his second term, including the bombing of Libya, the Iran–Iraq War, the Iran–Contra affair, and the ongoing Cold War. In June 1987, four years after he publicly described the Soviet Union as an "evil empire", Reagan challenged Soviet General Secretary Mikhail Gorbachev to "tear down this wall!", during a speech at the Brandenburg Gate. He transitioned Cold War policy from détente to rollback by escalating an arms race with the USSR while engaging in talks with Gorbachev. The talks culminated in the INF Treaty, which shrank both countries' nuclear arsenals. Reagan began his presidency during the decline of the Soviet Union, which ultimately collapsed nearly three years after he left office. When Reagan left office in 1989, he held an approval rating of 68%. From Wikipedia

I was a Chemical Dependency Counselor in Colstrip, Montana, and Lyle was employed by the school system as a Custodian. Farming had been such a challenge so he sold his farm, and made the move to a steady job with good benefits. My job did not offer benefits.

1990's

Montana Power share holders lose! Montana Power was owned by thousands of shareholders. With the arrival of utility deregulation in the 1990s, Montana Power restructured itself into a telecommunications company, Touch America Holdings, and began divesting its utility and energy holdings. The company built a 21,000-mile (34,000 km) fiber optics network and incurred heavy losses during the dot-com downturn in the early 2000s. Touch America filed for Chapter 11 bankruptcy protection in 2003, selling its facilities to 360 networks with plans to sell off remaining assets to defend against shareholder lawsuits. Litigation over the company's assets continued until early 2013, when a settlement was reached offering shareholders 29 cents per share. The shares were once worth $65.

The Internet opened up an entire new world. And there were Wars everywhere! The United States had been involved in the Gulf War. Civil War in Afghanistan of 1992-1996. Yugoslavia was also involved in war.

George Herbert Walker Bush (June 12, 1924 – November 30, 2018) was an American politician, diplomat, and businessman who served as the 41st president of the United States from 1989 to 1993. He was President Reagan's Vice President. His promise of "No New Taxes," that he broke, lost his 2nd term to Clinton.

We all watched the Rodney King Trial in 1992. Racial tensions surfaced between the police and the Blacks.

Then in 1995, we watched the police chase O.J. Simpson for miles after the murder of his ex- wife and her friend; he was found innocent although few really believed so.

Bill Clinton was elected President in 1992. In his first term as the president, Clinton signed the North American Free Trade Agreement into law. While this was popular with big business, it was very unpopular with those that saw their jobs going to China and Mexico.

We supported Ross Perot. The "giant sucking sound" was United States presidential candidate Ross Perot's phrase for what he believed would be the negative effects of the North American Free Trade Agreement (NAFTA), which he opposed.

Clinton did win a second term in 1996, but was impeached in 1998. His impeachment arose after he denied having an affair with a White House intern, Monica Lewinsky. The stained dress of Monica Lewinsky made the news until the hearing was over.

Though the House of Representatives voted to impeach Clinton, he was acquitted of all charges by the Senate.

In 1993, President Clinton and Janet Reno were responsible for the deaths of women and children in Waco, and Ruby Ridge occurred where a pregnant woman was shot by the ATF. I was so upset by both!

The Waco siege, also known as the Waco massacre, was the law enforcement siege of the compound that belonged to the religious sect Branch Davidians. It was carried out by the U.S. federal government, Texas state law enforcement, and the U.S. military, between February 28 and April 19, 1993. The Branch Davidians were led by David Koresh and were headquartered at Mount Carmel Center ranch in the community of Axtell, Texas, 13 miles northeast of Waco. Suspecting the group of stockpiling illegal weapons, the Bureau of Alcohol, Tobacco, and Firearms obtained a search warrant for the compound and arrest warrants for Koresh, as well as a select few of the group's members.

The incident began when the ATF attempted to serve a search and arrest warrant on the ranch. An intense gunfight erupted, resulting in the deaths of four government agents and six Branch Davidians. Upon the ATF's entering the property and failure to execute the search warrant, a siege lasting 51 days was initiated by the Federal Bureau of Investigation . Eventually, the FBI launched an assault and initiated a tear gas attack in an attempt to force the Branch Davidians out of the ranch. Shortly thereafter, the Mount Carmel Center became engulfed in flames. The fire resulted in the deaths of 76 Branch Davidians, including 25 children, two pregnant women, and David Koresh himself. From Wikipedia

Ruby Ridge was the site of an eleven-day siege in 1992 in Boundary County, Idaho, near Naples. It began on August 21, when deputies of the United States Marshals Service (USMS) initiated action to apprehend and arrest Randy Weaver under a bench warrant after his failure to appear on firearms charges. Weaver's wife, Vicki, was killed by FBI sniper fire.

From Wikipedia.

These incidents didn't help Clinton and Attorney General, Janet Reno's, reputations. For one thing they could have nabbed David Koresh when he went to town. They didn't ! This could have taken place long before the siege.

And with Ruby Ridge, was it necessary to shoot a pregnant woman?

Randy Weaver was under a bench warrant after his failure to appear on firearms charges. Given three conflicting dates for his court appearance, and suspecting a conspiracy against him, Weaver refused to surrender along with members of his immediate family, and family friend Kevin Harris, resisted as well. The Hostage Rescue Team of the Federal Bureau of Investigation became involved as the siege developed.

During the USMS reconnoiter of the Weaver property, six U.S. Marshals encountered Harris and Weaver's 14-year-old son, Sammy, in the woods near the family cabin. A shootout took place. Deputy U.S. Marshal William Francis Degan, Sammy Weaver, and the Weavers' dog, Striker, all died as a result. In the subsequent siege of the Weaver residence, led by the FBI, Weaver's wife Vicki was killed by FBI sniper fire. All casualties occurred in the first two days of the operation. The siege and standoff were ultimately resolved by civilian negotiators. Harris surrendered and was arrested on August 30, while Weaver and his three daughters surrendered the next day.

Weaver and Harris were subsequently arraigned on a variety of federal criminal charges, including first-degree murder for the death of Degan. Harris was acquitted of all charges, and Weaver was acquitted of all charges except for the original bail condition, a violation for the firearms charges and for missing his original court date. He was fined $10,000 and sentenced to eighteen months in prison, credited with time served plus an additional three months, and released after sixteen months.

During the federal criminal trial of Weaver and Harris, Weaver's attorney Gerry Spence made accusations of criminal wrongdoing against the agencies involved in the incident, in particular the FBI, the USMS, the Bureau of Alcohol, Tobacco, and Firearms (ATF), and the United States Attorney's Office (USAO) for Idaho. At the trial's end, the Department of Justice's Office of Professional Responsibility formed the Ruby Ridge Task Force (RRTF) to investigate Spence's charges. A redacted HTML version of the RRTF report, publicly released by Lexis Counsel Connect, raised questions about all the participating agencies' conduct and policies. The Justice Department later posted a more complete PDF version .

Both the Weaver family and Harris brought civil suits against the federal government over the firefight and siege. The Weavers won a combined out-of-court settlement in August 1995 of $3.1 million. After numerous appeals, Harris was awarded a $380,000 settlement in September 2000. From Wikipedia

The March 1998 issue from the Pew Research Center showed a definite change in how people viewed the government.

"Worry about the moral health of American society is suppressing satisfaction with the state of the nation, just as discontent with the honesty of elected officials is a leading cause of distrust of government. In the broadest sense, these ethical concerns are now weighing down American attitudes as Vietnam, Watergate, double digit inflation and unemployment once did.

Disillusionment with political leaders is essentially as important a factor in distrust of government as is criticism of the way government performs its duties. Cynicism about leaders is especially critical to distrust among the generations of Americans who came of age during and after the Vietnam and Watergate eras, while performance failures are more important to older Americans."

"Distrust of government and discontent with the country notwithstanding, there is no indication that these attitudes are near a crisis stage. Public desire for government services and activism has remained nearly steady over the past 30 years. And distrust of government is not fostering a disregard for the nation's laws, eroding patriotism or discouraging government service. About as many people would recommend a government job to a child today as would have in the early 1960s, when there was much less distrust of government."

My belief is America changed with the assassination of President John F. Kennedy. Then the wars, and with the internet, the secrets that had been kept of politicians behaviors, were brought to the forefront. How they voted, their illegitimate affairs, and the payoffs from lobbyists. The criminal actions of many of our politicians continued but the internet has given people a very distrusting and poor opinion of our leaders.

2000's

Many of us didn't think the world would still be here when 2000 rolled around. But it came with little fan fare. George Bush , son of George Herbert Walker Bush, was elected President.

On September 11, 2001, 19 militants associated with the Islamic extremist group al Qaeda hijacked four airplanes and carried out suicide attacks against targets in the United States. Two of the planes were flown into the twin towers of the World Trade Center in New York City, a third plane hit the Pentagon just outside Washington, D.C., and the fourth plane crashed in a field in Shanksville, Pennsylvania. Almost 3,000 people were killed during the 9/11 terrorist attacks.

The hijackers were Islamic terrorists from Saudi Arabia and several other Arab nations. Reportedly financed by the al Qaeda terrorist organization of Saudi fugitive Osama bin Laden, they were allegedly acting in retaliation for America's support of Israel, its involvement in the Persian Gulf War, and its continued military presence in the Middle East.

Some of the terrorists had lived in the United States for more than a year and had taken flying lessons at American commercial flight schools. Others had slipped into the country in the months before September 11 and acted as the "muscle" in the operation.

The 19 terrorists easily smuggled box-cutters and knives through security at three East Coast airports and boarded four early-morning flights bound for California, chosen because the planes were loaded with fuel for the long transcontinental journey. Soon after takeoff, the terrorists commandeered the four planes and took the controls, transforming ordinary passenger jets into guided missiles.

The 9/11 attacks had an immediate negative effect on the U.S. economy. Many Wall Street institutions, including the New York Stock Exchange, were evacuated during the attacks. On the first day of trading after the attacks, the market fell 7.1 percent, or 684 points. New York City's economy alone lost 143,000 jobs a month and $2.8 billion wages in the first three months. The heaviest losses were in finance and air transportation, which accounted for 60 percent of lost jobs. The estimated cost of the World Trade Center damage is $60 billion. The cost to clean the debris at Ground Zero was $750 million.

Thousands of first responders and people working and living in lower Manhattan near Ground Zero were exposed to toxic fumes and particles emanating from the towers as they burned and fell. By 2018, 10,000 people were diagnosed with 9/11-related cancer.

My thoughts on September 11, 2001: I sat glued to the TV as I watched the Twin Towers burn, and people jump to their deaths to avoid being burned to death. And I Cried Many Tears ! I had never seen anything like this, and all the people that were dying as I watched!

The one deed that President Bush did, I will always wonder why: he made arrangements to fly the Bin Laden family out of the United States before the ash even settled at the World Trade Center. WHY??

President Trump was elected in 2016. This sent shock waves through Hillary Clinton and her organization. They were so sure of winning they had their big Bash all planned. From that hour, President Trump's life would never be the same. Accusations, impeachment trials, etc. were constant, and the Media was no friend of Donald J.

Trump after he was elected. When he was a rich businessman, the Media swooned over him.

On July 29, 2019, President Trump signed a law authorizing support for the September 11 Victim Compensation Fund through 2092. Previously, administrators had cut benefits by up to 70 percent as the $7.4 billion fund depleted. Vocal lobbyists for the fund included Jon Stewart, 9/11 first responder John Feal, and retired New York Police Department detective, and 9/11 responder Luis Alvarez, who died of cancer 18 days after testifying before Congress.

My uncle, Fred Poloson, passed away February 18, 2004. His wife, Ann, had passed in 2000.

They were both laid to rest in the Lonepine Cemetery.

My daughter, Robin Rae, passed from Multiple Sclerosis February 19, 2006. Lyle and I went to California, and brought her ashes home so they could be inured at Lonepine. I cried for days. The grief I felt was so deep I can't even describe it.

My mother, Marie Poloson passed away December 20, 2008 at the age of 85. She was laid to rest at the Lonepine Cemetery next to my daughter, Robin Rae. When Mom died we were in the middle of a blizzard so I asked my sister to postpone her memorial; this was held at the Lonepine Hall in July of 2009.

Lyle had successful knee and shoulder replacements; his knee January of 2001. His shoulder February 2009.

Lyle had retired from the school January 1, 2001. I was still counseling, and we were raising Tennessee Walking Horses; also selling horses for others. I am proud of selling a Palomino Mare to Israel, and a Black Mare to the Netherlands. We enjoyed the foals so much. Lyle and I also spent a lot of time with our saddle horses in the Big Horn Mountains of Wyoming. One of God's Special Creations.

We traveled to Idaho, Washington, Oregon, California, Nevada, and Arizona. We visited the Grand Canyon, Yosemite, The San Diego Zoo, Sea World, Yellowstone Park, Glacier Park, Jackson Hole, Wyoming,Craters Of the Moon, and the Pryor Wild Horse Range. So many places, and to be able to share those with Lyle was a Blessing.

Lyle Vernon "Bud" Larson passed away December 16, 2013, and took my heart with him. It is now 2021, and I still miss him so much. He does come to me in dreams for which I am blessed & thankful. He will always be "My Handsome Brown Eyed Man."

I was writing the book, "An Immigrant A Homesteader And Sheep" before Lyle's passing. We had traveled to Polson to interview my Uncle Bert and Aunt Fay. I finished the book a year after Lyle's death, and a month before Uncle Bert's death.

When I found all the letters Lyle had saved of our courtship another book came to be, "Once In A Lifetime Comes A Man." Then I remembered I had written "The Making Of A Con" when I was in college. Those two were self published, the same as the Immigrant book.

The 21st of July 2019, brought about my youngest son, Dan's, passing. Again the deep pain of losing a child. My son, Kevin, and I drove to Dixon, California for Dan's military funeral. Dan's family was devastated, 3 adult children and his widow. The blessing as I write this, is Dan's family moved to Spokane, Wa. His oldest stayed in California, but having the others so close is such a blessing.

On November 22, 2019, Aunt Fay passed away. That was my 79th birthday! Fay had been like a Mom to me when I was a child. Fay & Grandma Mae Poloson were so special to me. Fay's husband, Bill, had passed in May of 1975, a year before Grandpa Dan Poloson's passing. Fay's passing prompted another book, "Fay," when I found so many of her stories in a trunk stored in her basement.

2021

The Trump Presidency was replaced by Joe Biden in 2021. I know for a fact there was so much fraud; when I went to bed on November 3, 2020, President Trump had been so far ahead. When I scanned the results the next morning Biden was the winner ! I was just sick over what had happened. President Trump, as far as I am concerned rates as one of the best Presidents we have ever had.

Lyle had wanted Trump to run in 2011. He said Trump was the only one who could beat the Clinton Machine. 2016 proved Lyle right. But the Left was not going to give up; they were going to be in office no matter what, and they succeeded, I am sad to say.

So 2021 starts with Biden at the helm and Obama in the background. Almost all of Obama's appointees are now in the Biden Presidency.

The Keystone Pipeline was Biden's 1st victim. Next came the rest of the, very good for our country, orders Trump had signed, being done away with by a stroke of Biden's pen, or maybe his wife's since his dementia is getting much worse. 1000's of people were put out of work, but next a check of $1400 would go out to the Masses. What better way to calm the people who

are out of work. COVID was used as the reason, and so many small businesses had to shut down.

Now Afghanistan has been given over to the Taliban after 20 years and all of our young military personnel's blood. The Afghan people are already being captured, murdered, and the women raped, or worse. Speaker Pelosi made the comment, "the Taliban have to give the women a seat at the table." Is she crazy ? The women will be treated cruelly, and many will end up murdered.

The Afghan men and women have been clinging to our planes and helicopters , trying to escape the Taliban. The Afghan President caught the 1st plane available. Biden's Inept, General Milley, has sent Marines to rescue Americans from the Embassy; the Taliban already control it.

President Trump had a plan for bringing our troops home, and it sure would not have happened like this. At the first actions by the Taliban a few bombs would have been dropped. President Trump never would have allowed the Taliban takeover, and our citizens' lives to be endangered.

And President Biden and his press secretary have gone on vacation ! So closes one half of 2021. I guess we will see. I am not at all optimistic. My prayers are for the people of Afghanistan and our Military & Embassy Personnel.

As this is happening Iran is flexing its war powers, and so is Russia. We are now buying oil from the Mideast since Biden has made sure we are no longer Energy Independent. Israel is under attack by Hezbollah again, and their newly elected Prime Minister isn't near as tough as Netanyahu was.

Our border with Mexico is wide open under Biden. 1000's are crossing into the United States. The MS 13 gang members, drugs, sex trafficking of women and children, and COVID ! We The People are expected to get the vaccine, wear masks, etc. but this country is wide open for the illegals.

We are also told we must get the vaccine; some businesses are mandating this, and our government would like nothing better than to mandate that we all have to take this vaccine.

It has gone through ZERO testing and many doctors, including a Mayo Clinic Pathologist, have expressed concern, and he has shown the harmful effects on the brain, heart, and immune system of these vaccines. The most frightening is vaccinating our Military Personnel. These are all young men and women, and so far the vaccines have caused some very serious side affects among these young people such as Myocardial infarction, sterility, miscarriages, and who knows what future effects will show up.

Now Farmers are asked to destroy their crops and oil is being dumped onto the ground! What is the plan for the people of this world? Starvation? Wars?

I will be 90 when 2030 rolls around. It is anyone's guess what that will bring. Will we be pushing our cars because there isn't any fuel, or because they don't have the computer components that operate the automobiles? Will we be living in cold homes because the electric grid is no longer operable? Will there be enough food since farmers need gasoline and diesel to operate their farm machinery. Where will they bury all the Solar Fields and Wind Towers that are killing our birds and bees?

Or maybe, my Grandmother's prediction that I will live to enjoy the 1000 Years Of Peace will come to pass, and with the earth cleansed of Evil, we won't have to worry about all of these things.

The Lord said He will bring to ruin those ruining his earth, and He also said that the earth will stand to time indefinite. For all of the suffering of people throughout history, this Paradise will be a God Send ! Will I live to see it come to pass?

Post Cards & Letters

I COULD NOT THINK OF A way to protect and keep these old family post cards and letters other than to add them to this book.

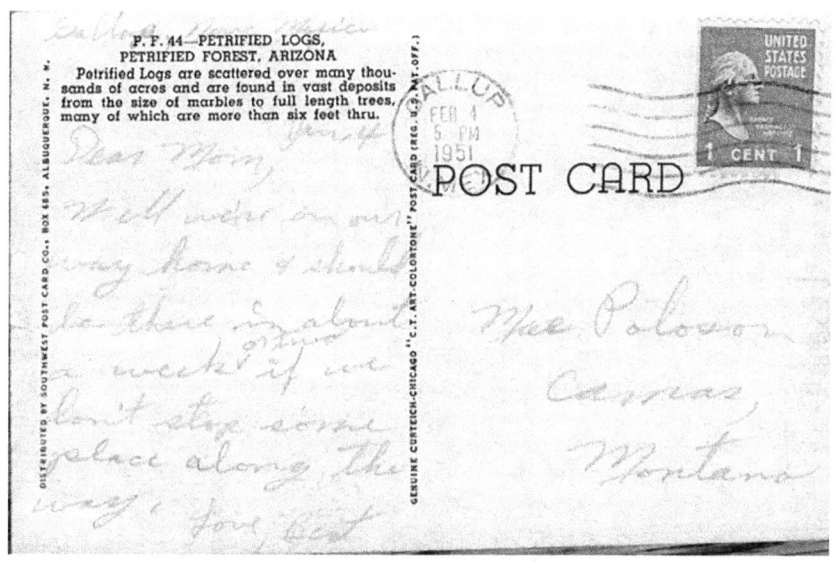

From Bert Polson to his mother, my Grandmother.

Next is Bert's letter to his sister, Fay Polson (Haynes) when he was packing horses and mules in Yellowstone Park.

Next is Fred Polson's letter to Fay, his sister. Fred and Bert are my Uncles, my Mother's brothers.

Old Faithful
July, 10

Dear Ray,

Well I'm here at Old Faithful without much to do so will write a few lines.

I got a letter from Lucille & she said the Kootenai wants Fred & I both next year. I may try it a year. Don't know till fall how I'll come out here. They may make a good job for me but doubt it. I'm making 312 bucks every 4 weeks now & not doing much either. I brought my six mules down here from Mammoth pk. dist. They're not bad mules but these are pretty nervous. I'm supposed to have them gentle by fall. All I have to do is pack a six man trail crew. We are going out maybe this week on a three day circle & then we're going out for

maybe the rest of the season
I'll stay right in the camp but
will be out about twice a week for
grub. Don't know how you would
find me if you came.

Glad to hear your horses are
o.k. I told you then every one is
a good horse. Say hows Bert Martins
horse. I'm almost afraid to ask but
would sure like to know how he's
making out with him

I ~~was to~~ was over to Red Lodge
~~this Sunday~~. Sure a pretty drive. That
road goes up to 10,942 feet. There's
~~some lakes there all frozen over yet.~~
That girl went with me too. She
is the chief engineers daughter
& I want to get in good with him &
get a soft job driving truck. Jake
& I talked to her in Gardiner last
fall. She was cooks helper at
Madison road camp where I was

for a couple weeks. Sure a nice girl & lots of fun but just a good friend. Her name is Betty Wahlbrandt so if you come down look her up. She'll probably be at Lake from now on. There's a ~~road~~ camp there.

We were way up in the Teton the other day on horses. That's sure pretty country. We rode over snow thirty feet deep. Boy that's sure pretty country. Just as pretty as Glacier.

Well the boss was down yesterday & he thinks I'm sure doing a good job on the mules. He was chief ranger at Glacier during the war. He's sure a good guy to work for too.

I suppose Ned will be going to the ~~Kootenai~~ as soon as he can.

seen about all the country around here now.

If you come down you can find out where I'm at but sometimes I don't come out for a couple days. I come out every tues for grub & go back and also a week from the 28th I come out with timeslips & every two weeks after that. In a couple weeks were moving back eight or ten miles more so I won't be out much.

Hows Dad getting along. I'll have to write & see. Tell Mom hello, also Phil & Lucille. I got a letter from Lucille a month ago & ain't wrote yet but will when I get time. Betty is down at West Plumb & will know where I'm at & when I'm coming out if you come. Well so long for now

Bert

Grace Larson

Yellowstone Park Wyo
Box 74   Dec 1, 1950

Dear Fay;

Got your letter a couple days ago. No Elk moving out of the Park yet. They are closer to the line now than they were the 1 irst of the year last winter. There is about 20 or so head out at Blacktail about 10 miles out. I was out to the Gold Brick ranch (Buffalo ranch) yesterday + saw a lot of Elk. Water Edge toward Hell Roaring creek they there is another big bunch. When Bert comes back down you'd better come along. Today I shod down at Gardiner not much shoeing now. Wouldn't be over it head every 6 weeks if they didn't have a bunch of Sears Roebuck Cowboys here. Condie says Shoe the little team we don't need the big team. Mother Jim says the little team is too Goddamn Small. Mother Jim turns his back So I shoe the little team for Condie, Condie goes to sleep in the manger so I shoe the big team for Mother Jim awhile Condie Snores.

The World here is good the Ship is pretty good. Nobody bothers me.

We have a bunch four inches of Snow here, by We I mean the rangers, The rest of us don't get any because we never went to School long enough.

They're having a hell of a time with the elk here. They got a guy riding herd on them, they give him the job rather than shoot him. He counts the elk & then counts the grass to see if they need more grass or more elk. This year they got too much grass so they got to pull it & put it up in trees so the elk can't reach it. They got to catch all the elk & give them each a shot of raw linseed oil. They're kind of bound up from eating too much.

This is quite a place down here you should come down & see the lay out. don't stay too long.

you might get goofy & start counting grass yourself. They take these rangers out & picket them by the necks so they can count grass. If they don't picket them they get over in the other guys grass & both of them forget their count. Theres a few they got to picket by a hind foot. They got rubber necks & get to far away from their stake.

If Bert cares come along Its a pritty warm country down here. I got a good house, water trough, spring, every thing you need.

So you Fred

From Grandma Mae Poloson's Memory Box

Announcing the arrival of Alice Mae McBroon
On July 23 '43
Weight 7½ lbs
Mr. & Mrs. Obe McBroon

The stork dropped in
the other day
And right away
we thought
You might be
kind of interested
In knowing
what he brought

Name Kevin Leo Bach

Arrived July 22 1:00 AM

Weight 8 lbs. ½ oz. 20½ in

Parents Mr. and Mrs. Leo Bach

Dusk Till Dawn in the Wild World

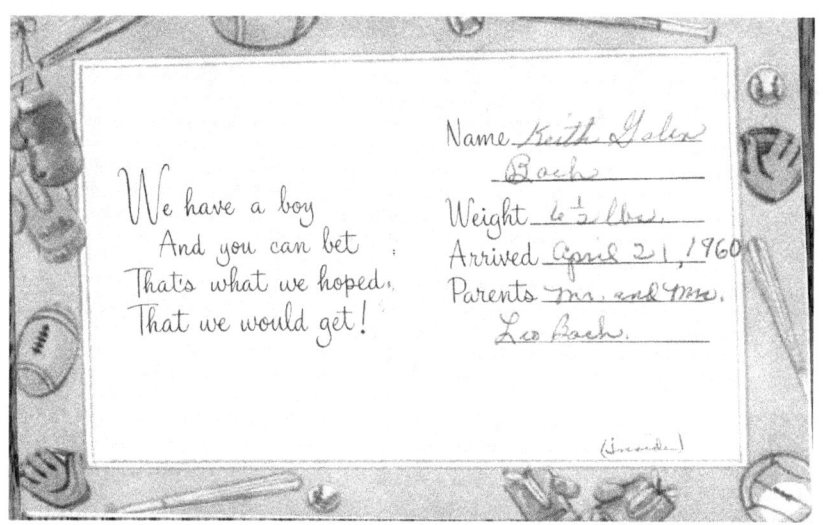

*Grandma Mae's letter with family history–
Indian Territory–AR-OK Border*

GRACE LARSON

When my married sister lived at Gowan, a mining town not far from Hartshorne, Indian Territory, my younger brother went to stay with her while he worked at the coal mines. When he came home, he told us of 3 ways of peddling whiskey, that are not mentioned in this story.

One bootlegger had a hollow walking cane and would unscrew the cap on the tip of the cane, and sell a yard of whiskey or any part of a yard that a man wanted.

Another had refillable zinc collars on his horses and would uncap the openings and sell a drink or a collar

> full of whiskey
> One man, politely wheeling
> a baby buggy for his wife(?) could
> reach under the blankets and
> hand out a bottle and
> then tip the hood of the buggy
> low again "to keep the sun out
> of the baby's eyes." That way, it
> wasn't so easy to see they had
> forgotten to bring the baby.
> And, of course, the common name
> "bootlegger" was the naturally
> chosen name for the one who
> carried flat sided bottles
> in his bootlegs.
>   M. Poloson

*Grandma Mae's note about a DeSchamps that
as wounded in the 2nd World War*

> Joseph DesChamps of Limoges France
> carried rifle slug in his ~~bad~~ liver from
> War in 1940 (second World War) Item in Grit News
> section, page 42, May 15, 1966

GRACE LARSON

Family Post Cards

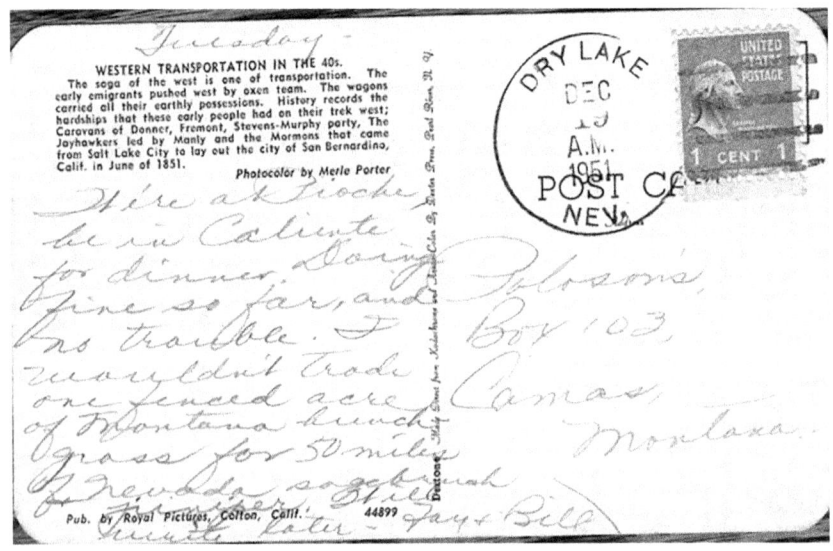

*From Fay and Bill on their honeymoon
trip. Fay Poloson Haynes now.*

The letter below is from Bert to Fay when he was packing horses and mules in Yellowstone Park. I don't have the ending!

> Old Faithful
> July 29
>
> Dear Fay,
> I thought I'd better write & let you know I'm still here & okay.
> We haven't got far. The camp is about 12 miles from Old Faithful. I've been back & forth most every day or two. I stay one night here & one in the trail camp. We'll be there maybe two weeks yet. The foreman is having trouble with his crew of college boys. Every week two go in & he sends two out.
> Boy the mosquitoes & horse flys are sure bad here. Worst I ever seen.
> This is last night & I'm going to West Yellowstone. It used to be pretty lively but they stopped all the gambling. Was over to Cody last turn. I've

From Bert & Betty; they will be taking the trail ride down into the Grand Canyon.

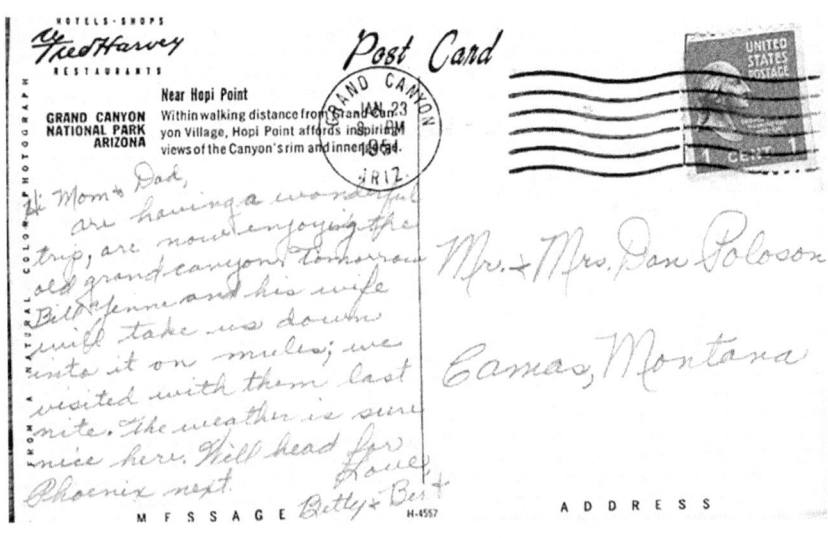

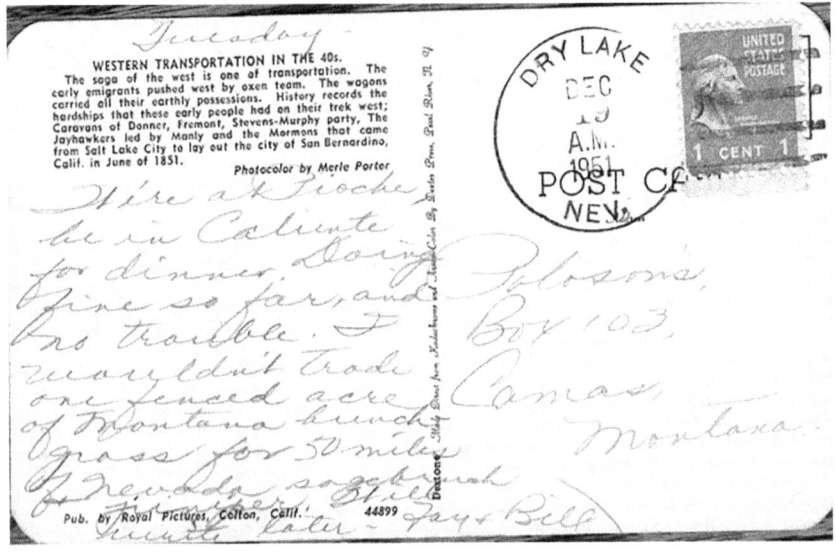

Dusk Till Dawn in the Wild World

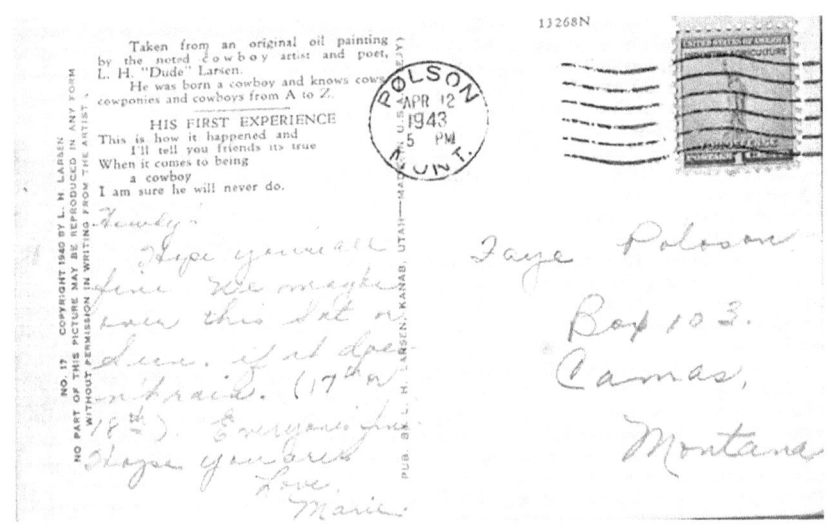

To Fay from my mother, Marie Poloson McBroom

    The above cards are from Fred when he was working in Idaho and then Alaska.

The Poloson Place - 1929

QUILLIGAN place.

This is what the Poloson place looked like when Dan and Mae bought it in 1929. They eventually moved the Carlin House next to this one so there would be bedrooms for Fred and Bert. When they piped water from the upper spring, Grandma Mae had a faucet right by her front door.

Epilogue

WHEN THIS BOOK IS PUBLISHED, my focus will be piano, volunteering, and sending photos to Lyle's niece, Donna. I have no plans for another book.

I have hired a Screenwriter for "Once In A Lifetime Comes A Man." My granddaughter, Gin, did research on Anne xu, and her findings were all positive, so I hired Anne to write the Screenplay. This is a chance I have to take. Sony Pictures had contacted me in May, but I didn't have an agent or anything at that time.

My computer can take a rest now, and I will begin a new direction filled with all sorts of possibilities. Writing has been an amazing gift; a way to remember; a way to express; a way to acknowledge the Special People that have been in my life, and those that are still with me on this beautiful earth. And most of all, A Thanks To God, Our Creator, For The Blessing Of Life.

www.ingramcontent.com/pod-product-compliance
Lightning Source LLC
LaVergne TN
LVHW011725060526
838200LV00051B/3029